This Tarnished Light

by

Laura Strickland

This Tarnished Light

Cover Art by *Diana Carlile*

The Wild Rose Press, Inc.
PO Box 708
Adams Basin, NY 14410-0708
Visit us at www.thewildrosepress.com

Publishing History
First Edition, 2022
Trade Paperback ISBN 978-1-5092-4185-9
Digital ISBN 978-1-5092-4186-6

Published in the United States of America

But I find it hard even now to describe Albert's eyes. For neither their color nor their shape made them so remarkable. I've seen a few other people during my life who had what Albert had. For those people carry a light—one which neither pain nor hardship can successfully dim, at least not for long.

That's what I saw when I looked into Albert's eyes that afternoon—flickering light, like the sun on water, like hope, like belief there was something beyond the want and endurance.

Of course I didn't realize all that then. I remember hoping he wouldn't call all the other boys over to me, 'cause I'd seen them gather round some hapless victim before to beleaguer him or her just for fun.

So I merely stared at him and tried to shrink farther into my corner.

"Wot's your name?" he asked. He told me later, much later, he decided then—right at that moment—I was the girl he would marry. Even though I was not quite twelve, and he but fourteen.

I found the light in his eyes irresistible. It danced. It possessed its own magic, like music, and it seemed to surround and uplift me.

"Polly Bridger," I whispered.

"Well, Polly Bridger." He repeated it as if burning it into his memory. "I'm Albert Coward. You need anything, you come to me, right?"

Praise for Laura Strickland

Laura Strickland's novella *FORGED BY LOVE* won first place in the short historical category of the International Digital Awards. Her book *STEAM TINKER* part of her Buffalo Steampunk Adventure series, won the 2021 NNLight Award for Science Fiction.

~*~

"The world building is phenomenal."

~Daysie W. at My Book Addiction and More

~*~

"Laura Strickland creates a world that not only draws you in, but she incorporates it…seamlessly.…the kind of book that keeps you awake well into the wee hours, and sighing with satisfaction when you've finished the very last page."

~Nicole McCaffrey, Author

~*~

"As I read I became so involved with the story, I found it difficult to put down the book.…Definitely…an author to watch."

~Dandelion at Long & Short Reviews

~*~

"Laura Strickland takes us beyond the fairy tale and ballroom and gives the readers a story full of pain and heartbreak, wonderfully balanced with hope and love."

~Elissa Blabac, InD'tale Magazine

~*~

"What follows will make you cry, angry, and appreciative of your own life."

~Lisa O'Connor, Author and Reviewer

Dedication

To all the Polly Bridgers who have ever lived.
You are beautiful, every one.

Chapter One

London, Spitalfields, Autumn 1854

It's peaceful here, and quiet considering how many others lie so close around me. I can feel them in that funny, distant way you feel your leg after it goes asleep on you. I feel an arm here, a foot there. Somebody's chest lies just beneath my left shoulder. We are stretched in rows one atop the other, like cordwood stacked in the old gunnel, back home.

I can't rightly remember how long it's been since I knew peace. My gran, who died more than ten year ago now, used to say peace came to a joyful heart. But it's hard to have a joyful heart when you don't know where your next meal's coming from, and you've no place to lay your head.

I had a good life, once. When I was younger, Ma, Pa, my little sister, Mary, and I lived in two nice rooms in Champher's Close, East London. Pa had a good job then, making dolls out of our house. Ma would help him to finish them, sewing them beautiful dresses, and even I helped clean the molds in spite of being so young. Mary couldn't help, her being just a babe in arms. But we always had enough to eat and could pay the rent.

That's real important, innit? Being able to pay the rent. For a time, it ruled my life and got me into the terrible way I was forced to make my living. Even above an empty belly, the rent held supreme importance. And I feared not having a place, I can't deny I did.

Later, when I met Darcy, she taught me that was the fault of my grand early upbringing. I'd never had to sleep in the gutter as thousands did, nor even, if I was lucky, in a doorway. I'd been spoiled by my easy childhood, coddled even. She taught me there were folk in London who never knew the security of a roof over their heads, so couldn't miss it.

I never disagreed with Darcy about much—maybe I should have. But lying here now in the quiet, I think Darcy was wrong about this one thing. It comforts me, remembering that once I was loved. I cherish the memory of our little two rooms and being tucked into my own bed at night by loving hands…

…no matter how far from me that memory now seems.

The downfall of our family started with Pa getting sick. It didn't seem much at first, just a bit of dizziness and a bad stomach. He started to throw up what he ate, but Ma said it would pass.

When he got the sweats and couldn't rise from his bed, Ma took over casting the heads, hands, and feet for the dolls. But when the doll merchant, Mr. Crandal, came, he said the dolls were faulty and refused to pay. He still charged us for the supplies we used, though, the wax and the cloth to make the bodies.

"Make the next ones perfect," he told Ma when he left. And we tried, we truly did. We melted the wax just the way Papa always did, the stink of it filling both rooms, all while Pa lay in the bed breathing through his open mouth so loud you could count each breath, like the harsh rattle of coal down a chute.

I do not know what went wrong with that next batch of dolls. Perhaps we did not get the temperature high enough. I just remember how tired we were, how foggy I felt in my head, and the aching in my limbs. There seemed to be no air in our rooms, and Mary in her cot mewled weakly.

When the faces, hands, and feet came out of the molds, they crumbled. Ma sat and wept over them in despair.

"What are we to do?" she asked. I did not think she asked me as such, even though she used my name. "What shall we do, Polly?" For that's my name, Polly Bridger.

I wished I could make it better—for her and for Pa and Mary—even though in my heart I knew she called upon some higher power, perhaps the one Gran used to call Our Holy Father. Whomever she called upon besides me, he did not listen. The wax pieces we needed so desperately remained crumbled, and Papa did not miraculously rise from his bed to make things right.

Many a time since have I wondered if that entity upon whom Ma called exists. I have been up the stairs, so to speak, and down them again with the matter. In my darkest moments when things seemed most hopeless, I've been sure there was no one to save me but myself. But there have been other, fleeting moments—oh, yes—when against the very worst odds I've felt uplifted. I've caught a glimpse of something—like a flicker of light—in the eyes of a person or in someone's smile...

But for the most part there's been only darkness.

Ma pulled herself together after a time. When Mr. Crandal next came, she showed him the ruined pieces and begged him to let her keep sewing the dresses, the clever little hats and bags for the dolls that other families might manufacture. For there were others like us, as I well knew.

"I have two children to keep," she fairly wept. "And I fear my husband is dying."

Mr. Crandal glanced at Papa, who lay senseless in the bed. So did I. As I understood it, people died every day—from tiny babes to elders. Gran had died. I hadn't thought that Pa might. Even though he now seemed unaware of us, he still dominated our existence. Ma spent what little free time she had coaxing him to drink water or broth and beseeching him to come awake.

"Best call a physician for him, woman," Mr. Crandal said.

"I cannot afford to." Ma twisted her fingers together. "I must keep my girls fed, and there's the rent—"

Mr. Crandal swept Ma with a look up and down again. "Then you'd best find another way to earn, had you not? You're a good-looking woman. I am sure you can think of something."

Ma paled before she flushed red. "I'm a respectable wife, Mr. Crandal, that I am, and a good seamstress."

"You're a fair hand with the needle, all right. But I need my dolls to be perfect. Did I not tell you and your husband so from the first? Do you think the children of Bloomsbury want shoddy, misshapen dollies?"

"No, sir."

"I will give you until tomorrow. If your husband is not on his feet by then, I will collect my supplies and you will no longer work for me. Understand?"

Ma nodded and twisted her hands together even harder. After Mr. Crandal left, she went to the bed and begged Pa to sit up and speak with her. I remember how his head flopped back on the pillow when she urged him to rise and how Mary set to wailing.

Mary wailed all night long. No matter how Ma beseeched him, Pa never woke. By the morning, he lay stiff and cold.

All Ma's tears dried up then. She sat clasping Pa's hand in both of hers, just staring at nothing as if she could see our future in the air. I tried to comfort Mary, who would not stop crying.

I didn't know then that Mary had fallen sick too. She felt warm to me, but then, little ones who cry often do turn red and feel heated.

After a time, one of the neighbors, Mrs. Best, came knocking. I answered the door, still with Mary in my arms, since Ma didn't seem to hear the knock.

Mrs. Best, a large, brisk woman, said to me, "Let me in, child. Has your father up and died, then?"

Ma had not said as much to me, but the long, difficult breaths that had filled the room and my ears had all ceased. I nodded.

She clicked her tongue. "Dear, dear." She went and spoke to Ma, who barely responded. Then she left.

Some men arrived a good while later and took Pa away. At Ma's insistence, they wrapped him in the sheet from the bed before they carried him out.

Later, when Mrs. Best returned with others of the neighbors, she scolded Ma for it.

"Giving up your good sheet for such a reason! You could have sold that. You will need the coin."

"I couldn't send him, couldn't send—" Ma's voice broke on the words.

Mrs. Best clicked her tongue again. "He won't mind, duck."

Everything changed at that moment when the men carried Pa out. Or maybe it all changed before that, when I stopped hearing those rasping breaths that had filled our days.

But I didn't know it then, not really. I thought Ma would manage somehow, would keep feeding us and maintain a roof over our heads.

Even when Mr. Crandal came back later that day and hollered at her, ordering her to gather up all the doll supplies, the dresses she'd already completed, squinting in the poor light as she sewed. And the last of the fabrics and lace, even the thread, leaving us nothing.

Nothing.

I still thought that somehow my life would continue on, more or less the same. Because I could imagine little else.

"Where have the men taken Papa?" I asked Ma, standing in front of her with my fingers tangled in my pinafore.

She roused enough to look at me. "To the paupers' yard."

"What's that?"

"A graveyard for those who cannot afford a proper burial."

I did not know the difference then between a proper burial and an improper one. But Ma reached out and clasped my fingers fiercely.

"Promise me, Polly, you'll never end up there. Promise you'll make something of yourself."

I had no idea what she meant, but I wanted to comfort her, so I nodded. I would have promised anything to ease the terrible pain I saw in her eyes.

Ironic, isn't it, given where I now lie? But I want you to know—and I want her to know wherever she may now be—I tried. I did strive to be the good girl she wanted me to be.

Sometimes in life we are presented with very few choices. I made mine the best that I could.

Chapter Two

When Mr. Grimp came, Ma tried to reason with him. Mr. Grimp was the landlord, and he wanted the rent, it being the first of the month. The only time we saw Mr. Grimp back then was when he wanted paying the rent. The rest of the time the ceiling might well fall in, or the toilet out in the yard might be overflowing, and we would not see the landlord.

I listened, juggling Mary in my arms and trying to keep her quiet while he and Ma shared a hushed conversation at the door. Mary rarely stopped crying, and her skin burned to the touch.

"Mr. Grimp, sir, if you could please to afford me just a bit more time—"

"I am not a charity, Mrs. Bridger."

"To be sure, I quite understand that. But I do not have all the rent."

"How much do you have?"

"Barely half. But sir, I would keep some of what I have back so I can feed my children."

"Your children, missus, are not my responsibility."

"Sir, my husband has just died—"

"Will your children be any less hungry out on the street?"

"No, sir. But if you could show us some—some generosity just until I find a job—"

"Generosity, is it?" A new note in his voice made

8

me swivel my head and stare. He swept Ma with a look up and down—one that made me prick all over with heat.

"You're a good-looking woman," he said, just as Mr. Crandal had. "Maybe we can come to an arrangement."

Ma fell silent.

After a long moment Mr. Grimp spoke again. "Of course if you'd rather bundle up your things and get out—"

She shook her head.

I have wondered since, after the truth of what happened next came to me, whether she refused what he asked of her with that shake of the head or refused the prospect of being cast out.

It must have been the last, for she went with him. After casting one burning look at me and bidding me keep Mary quiet, she led Mr. Grimp to the bed in the corner—the same where Pa had died—and pulled the curtains that screened it across so I could not see.

But I could *hear*. I could hear everything.

****

After that, Mr. Grimp came often. He and Ma always went directly to the bed behind the curtains. He never stayed long.

I wanted to ask Ma about it. I ached to ease the sick feeling in the pit of my stomach every time Mr. Grimp appeared at our door. I hoped she could reassure it away from me. But I could not quite bring myself to broach the matter. Ma never looked at me after he left. I thought maybe she tried to pretend it didn't happen.

Besides, other things demanded our attention. Our bellies stayed empty and so did the cupboards. The two factors later to rule my life—a roof and an empty belly—had already become paramount.

Ma went out most days looking for work but found none. I stayed back and looked after Mary.

By then neither of us could deny Mary was very sick. She still cried but only in a weak manner. She must be hungry, I knew, just like me. The poor mite had sucked her thumb till the skin went all chapped.

One day while Ma was out looking for work, I changed Mary's nappy to find her all covered in spots. I tried washing them off with a cool cloth—she seemed so hot all the time. And when Ma got home, I showed her.

Not much these days altered the dull look in Ma's eyes, but that seemed to. They blazed as she gathered Mary into her arms and cried to the very air, "No! You shall not take her, too."

That night when Mr. Grimp came, she said to him, "Mr. Grimp, sir, my baby is dying."

"All the more reason to keep a roof over her head, eh?"

"Sir, can you not show some mercy? I cannot face…with her ill…"

"What else do you have, woman, with which you might pay the rent?" Alarmingly, he turned his gaze on me. "Your daughter is very pretty. Maybe—"

"Sir, she is barely twelve years old. Never."

"Then you'd best give me what I ask. D'you know how much rent I could get for these two rooms?"

Ma went behind the curtains with him. Later, after he left, I crept in to find her lying there on her back as if broken, naked except for the blanket.

"Ma? Ma, are you sick?"

"Yes, Polly."

My world rocked around me. She could not be ill. I could not bear it.

"Ma, please get up."

She looked at me. She must have seen the tears in my eyes for she dragged herself up from the bed and put on her clothes.

I wondered what he did to her there behind the curtains, to put such a look on her face—as if everything had been burned away.

When I dredged up the courage to ask, some days later, she said, "Polly, there are times in life when you have to do things you do not want to do. Remember that—it is likely one of the most valuable lessons I will ever teach you."

Mary died three days later. At the end, Ma begged Mr. Grimp for coin so she might send for the doctor, but it was too late. Just like Pa, Mary's little body was carted away.

Ma did not weep.

****

After that I watched Ma fade. She had been pretty once—Pa never stopped telling her so—with hair the same yellow color as mine and blooming pink cheeks he likened to roses. He used to call me his little rose because I looked like her.

All that beauty seemed to drain from her the way water drains from a leaky bucket. There was no work, and we existed on almost nothing.

Mr. Grimp, deciding our two rooms were too grand for just a mother and daughter, moved us to a single room in another of his properties called Bishop's Close, a low place filled with low persons with whom Ma did not want to associate.

When she spurned them, they called her terrible names. One woman shouted, "I know how you pay your rent." The Close, tall and narrow, stank of the toilet and was never quiet.

I hated it there, but I knew now it was better than being on the streets. Ma must have known it also, for she kept trading to Mr. Grimp what he demanded.

When he came, and us with but the one room, I could not bear to listen, so I invariably took myself outside.

There I met others of the children, none better off than I. There I met Albert Coward, and a more inappropriate name I have yet to encounter. Not the Albert moniker—like thousands of other boys he'd been named after the Queen's husband. But he proved no coward, either then nor at any time after.

I will remember forever the first words he said to me. He was with some other boys playing in the yard, though the term *yard* proved inaccurate. The space, enclosed on all sides by tenements and with only a narrow alley for egress, had been paved in brick and not a single blade of grass grew there. The whole place stank of what was left in the toilets, and the sun—even when it shone in London, which was seldom enough— seemed afraid to peek in.

The game, noisy as always, proceeded to grow violent. The boys argued over a ball, or perhaps it was just a twist of rags they kicked about.

I had made myself as small as possible and pushed my way into one of the corners from where I might be able to see when Mr. Grimp left. I tucked my head down, wishing I were most anywhere else.

Suddenly he stood in front of me, a slim shadow blotting out the light.

"Cor, but you're pretty."

It made me lift my eyes to his face, lit in relief. I did not know if I'd seen him before, but I'd surely never noticed him.

Tall for his age and his station in life, Albert was also rail-thin, with elbows and knees poking out through his shabby clothes. He had ginger hair, a handsome face, and eyes that—

But I find it hard even now to describe Albert's eyes. For neither their color nor their shape made them so remarkable. I've seen a few other people during my life who had what Albert had. For those people carry a light—one which neither pain nor hardship can successfully dim, at least not for long.

That's what I saw when I looked into Albert's eyes that afternoon—flickering light, like the sun on water, like hope, like belief there was something beyond the want and endurance.

Of course I didn't realize all that then. I remember hoping he wouldn't call all the other boys over to me, 'cause I'd seen them gather round some hapless victim before to beleaguer him or her just for fun.

So I merely stared at him and tried to shrink farther into my corner.

"Wot's your name?" he asked. He told me later, much later, he decided then—right at that moment—I was the girl he would marry. Even though I was not quite twelve, and he but fourteen.

I found the light in his eyes irresistible. It danced. It possessed its own magic, like music, and it seemed to surround and uplift me.

"Polly Bridger," I whispered.

"Well, Polly Bridger." He repeated it as if burning it into his memory. "I'm Albert Coward. You need anything, you come to me, right?"

If I'd had any notion then of how many times I would do just that in the years to come, turn to him at the prompting of need or despair, asking the impossible—for him to save me—I might have marked the words more closely. As it was, I focused on the lads who called to him and looked likely to move our way.

Albert glanced over his shoulder at them and made a face. Then without another word he went away from me and joined them.

But he left some of his light.

Chapter Three

Winter came, and our suffering sharpened. Life in Bishop's Close only became more and more difficult. Rarely did Ma and I have coal for a fire, and the damp came right up through the walls and floor of the place. The very bricks seemed to weep damp.

My fingers turned wrinkled and purple, and my toes hurt all the time. Sometimes Mr. Grimp brought us a scuttle of coal, but I knew what Ma had to do for it and I couldn't enjoy its dubious warmth.

Ma tried hard to find work that winter, so she did. The most she ever got was a day or two's labor from which she returned barely able to stand from weariness. She said she'd got on the list for a job at the match factory and needed only to wait for an opening.

I didn't know then such openings occurred because the women and girls who worked there—some barely older than me—became too sick from the work to carry on.

My twelfth birthday came and went. Ma wept that day because she had no way to make me a birthday feast. In truth, our stomachs were more pinched than ever.

Some things did change, with me turning twelve. Mr. Grimp began looking at me differently when he came to visit. I did not like the way those glances made me feel, like I wanted to wash myself from head to foot.

Once I stood on the landing outside our room and heard him and Ma arguing about me.

"Your daughter's grown very pretty, Mrs. Bridger." He always called her that, *Mrs. Bridger*, though I understood by then he put his greasy hands all over her.

"No, absolutely not." Ma's voice sounded sharp.

"You haven't heard what I'm suggesting. Put the girl to work. She's well enough grown."

"She's a child!"

"No matter. There's a fancy for them young. A lot of men think a girl like her is the cure for French pox."

It was the first time I'd heard those words—*French pox*. I didn't understand what they meant, other than that *pox* indicated an illness.

Mr. Grimp continued to persuade in his high whine, "You could make a good bit o' coin."

"I suppose," Ma seethed with loathing, "you would bring the men in and take part of the earnings."

"Why not? She'll end up there anyway, if you keep on the way you are."

"She will not. I won't allow it. I do what I do for Polly's sake. Were it not for her, I would go throw myself in the river."

"Suit yourself, Mrs. Bridger."

He began moving then, making the grunting sounds that always accompanied his visits, and I took myself out into the cold yard.

Scarcely colder than our room.

We both nearly starved that winter, but it brought some changes. I began noticing that despite the fact we had no food, Ma grew stout rather than thinner.

When she caught me staring at her, she sat me

down at the rough little table in the center of our room and took my hands in hers.

"Polly, you will be wondering. I'm carrying Mr. Grimp's child."

I stared and tried to pull my fingers away. She looked unwell—pale and with new lines in her face— but most everyone I encountered looked like that. We lived like moles in our damp rooms and rarely saw daylight.

But I remember my sense of repugnance. Bad enough he touched her. She shouldn't have part of him inside her. For aye, I understood enough of it to grasp how babes came into the world. Plenty of them populated the Close.

I breathed, "No."

Her weary, blue eyes fled mine. "I am afraid so."

"What will we do?"

She shrugged. "Have it, I suppose."

"But we can't have a babe here. There's no room. It's too cold. We can barely feed ourselves."

"I know."

"You can't go out to work now," I wailed yet again. "What are we to do?"

This time she made no reply.

I said, "You will have to let me go out to work. I might get a place at the match factory."

"No."

"But we need—"

"Have you seen what happens to the girls who work there?"

By then, I had. I'd glimpsed the women on the streets—even here in the Close—and asked Ma why they went about with their shawls and kerchiefs wrapped around their faces.

She told me they worked at the factory and had contracted something called Fossy Jaw. The stuff they used to coat the matches made a kind of poison that came up and hit them in the face over and over again, day after day, and ate right through the skin into the bones.

"You would not want to see them without those cloths," she'd said.

"Does it hurt?"

"What do you think?"

I thought it would hurt unbearably, more than I could readily imagine. But it hurt also seeing the look in Ma's eyes. I wasn't sure having my jaw rot away would feel any worse.

"Maybe I could work there just a little while," I suggested. "Not long enough to get sick."

"No, Polly. I will take care of it."

I will admit, she tried. The next time Mr. Grimp came they talked about the arrival of his child.

"It is your responsibility," Ma told him. "We will need more coin."

"More, more, more. You women are all the same."

"Still, Mr. Grimp, there's no getting past the clear fact—"

"Get rid of it."

Ma gasped. "What?"

"You women know how, right?"

"I do not."

"There are others who do. Find out and get rid of it. Else you, your precious girl, and your brat will be out on the street."

Ma's voice shook when she said, "This is your

child, Mr. Grimp."

"Prove it," he sneered. "I don't know how many other men you've been granting favors, do I?"

"You're the only one."

"So you might well say. I have only your word for it. You point to me only because I've been so generous to you."

Generous? I nearly choked, hearing that.

"You want a roof over your head?"

"Yes, Mr. Grimp."

"Then you'll do as yer told."

That conversation took place just before Christmas. It proved a Christmas unlike any I'd ever known. Always in years past there'd been a bit of a feast. And presents for me and Mary—small things but exciting to receive, all the same.

Now with Pa and Mary gone, there was only hunger. Hunger and bare cupboards. I remember Ma weeping over it.

"I have nothing to feed you or this child, at Christmas."

I thought Mr. Grimp had told her to get rid of the child, but I did not say so. Ma cried more and more these days, and I did not want to set her off.

I felt like crying too, but I didn't want her to see me. I went outside. The weather that day proved just as bitter and cheerless as our room. Usually no matter the elements, the yard burgeoned with people. They overflowed from the crowded rooms and used this place for living space, especially the children.

But now it lay nearly empty. Two small boys sat crushed together on the far side, and a cat sniffed near the door of the toilet, which hung half open, swinging in the cold wind. Frost rimed the bricks of the buildings all around, and the cold bit right through my clothes.

I huddled up in my usual place and bent my head to hide my tears.

A voice said, "Happy Christmas, Polly Bridger."

I started and looked up straight into Albert Coward's eyes. Light danced in them—bright, golden light—and it reached out to enfold me like warmth.

Before I could speak, he asked, "Wot's wrong? Why you crying?"

It all came out then. It had been bottled far too long, and I had no one else to tell.

"We have nothing for our dinner, and it's Christmas, innit? And Ma's got Mr. Grimp's babe in her belly and won't be able to get hired even for a day job now, if she could find one."

He sat down beside me. A bad decision on his part, I thought. I could feel the cold and damp coming up from the ground.

But he didn't seem to notice. He said, "Mr. Grimp the landlord?"

I nodded.

He spoke a bad word but it was under his breath and not, I thought, aimed at me.

I wailed, "I don't know what we're going to do."

"Come, now. Some things are easily fixed, some not so much."

"Nothing is easily fixed."

"I can't do nothing about old Grimp. But if you come along of me, I can get you some dinner."

I stared into his eyes where the light abided. Perhaps, I thought, that was kindness I saw.

In my world, people were rarely kind. They kicked

dogs, played tricks on each other for entertainment, and bullied the weak. And Albert—he was one of the rough boys of Bishop's Close. Why should he be kind to me?

My mind—and stomach—focused on one word.

"Dinner?"

He smiled. Have I said that Albert Coward had a rare smile? It revealed a row of white teeth, all perfect save one which was chipped.

He held out his hand. "Come with me."

Why did I trust him? Trust was just as rare as kindness in the Close. And he might have had the worst of intentions.

Yet I put my hand in his and met the warmth of him, which felt very much like safety. And I let him lead me out into the Christmas morning.

Chapter Four

Beyond the Close lay another world. East London might share little with the West End—we saw no grand phaetons going by nor men in silk coats and top hats. But the neighborhood bustled. Plenty of folk populated the streets, hurrying through the bitter, falling snow.

And the wind came sharper here. Bishop's Close might well be a prison, but the same arms that enclosed could protect.

"Where are we going?" I asked Albert piteously.

"To buy yer dinner." His fingers felt so good on mine, so strong. So safe.

"What with? I haven't any money."

"I have."

"Where did you get money?"

He hesitated, and for the first time the light in his eyes dimmed a little. "I pick up a bit o' work from time to time. I have some pennies in my pocket."

I asked myself, would it be right to let him spend that coin, however earned, on me? Ma—and Pa before his death—had managed to impress some moral sense on me. One earned money and didn't accept charity.

But it was Christmas morning and my stomach ached with hunger, and Ma was up in our room crying.

Albert just might be an angel appeared to me.

My hand still in his, I tottered on the edge of the curb and clarified, "You mean to buy me dinner?"

"Yes."

"What do you want in return?"

He half frowned at me. "Nothin', Polly. It's a Christmas present."

A Christmas present. Just when I'd been certain I would receive none. Tears flooded my eyes.

"Here, don't go cryin' again."

"But you could spend that money on yourself."

"Don't want to."

"On your family."

"There's nobody except my brother, and he's away right now."

"The rent."

"I share with a load of other people, Polly." With his other hand, bare and not too clean, he touched my cheek. "I'd like to do this."

Objections continued to flow from me. "There won't be any place open today."

"I know a shop. Come on."

The shop when we reached it proved small and dimly lit, the sort you would walk right past on any other day. When Albert lifted the latch, the door opened and we went in.

The things he bought me that day were few—a bit of ham and half a loaf of bread, a twist of butter. To me it looked like wealth, a feast.

Stunned, I remained silent as we walked back to the Close where I turned and faced him.

"How can I thank you?"

He seemed to contemplate the question most seriously. I waited, watching snowflakes that looked like white feathers land on his ginger hair and wondering over again why he'd been so kind.

He said the last thing I expected. "Promise me something, Polly."

Here it comes, I thought, my stomach sinking with disappointment. There were strings attached after all to the parcel I clutched against my chest. He would make me promise to do something later that I might not want to do.

"What?" The word felt cold on my lips.

"Promise you'll remember to come to me if you're in trouble. I might be able to help."

That? Only that? I searched his eyes earnestly. I wanted so badly to reach for what he offered.

"Why?" I asked.

"Why, wot?"

"Why should you want to help me?"

"'Cause you're special, Polly Bridger. And I'm afraid you can't help yourself."

I cuddled the parcel more tightly. "So, we're…friends?"

"A friend's a good thing to have, yeah?"

I nodded.

"Happy Christmas, Polly," he said again.

"It will be, now. Because of you. Happy Christmas, Albert Coward."

I remember how the smile transfigured his face. He leaned in and kissed my cheek, his lips very gentle. It felt safe, warm.

"Remember your promise," he said.

I hadn't actually spoken a promise, but as I climbed the narrow stars to our room, I thought perhaps it was implicit with accepting his gift. And his kiss.

As I entered the room, I wondered how I could explain the feast to Ma. She lay face down on the bed.

For a moment I feared she was dead.

But when I touched her arm, she sat up. And when I showed her the bundle of food, she stared.

"Where did you get that?"

"It's a Christmas miracle."

"Did you steal it?"

"No, Ma. A gift."

"From whom?"

"From a friend."

I suppose we should have saved the food for later. Perhaps that's what Albert intended. Hunger would not allow it, and we downed it on the spot, all but a little bit I wrapped back up for tomorrow.

After that, Ma slept. I thought probably the babe in her belly made her tired. It seemed an unnatural sleep, though, and it lasted most the day.

I sat alone through that Christmas, wishing we had more coal for the fire and wondering what would become of us in the new year.

****

It did not take long for me to find out what was to become of us. Three days after Christmas, Mr. Grimp came. He and Ma argued again, and he threw some coins at her.

I'd seen Albert twice more by then. We took to meeting in my corner—that is, I would station myself there, and he would come and join me. He changed then. Though I'd seen him contesting and sparring with the other boys in the Close, he gentled when he came to me. We would sit and talk, just talk like two civilized people. Like two friends, I suppose.

I desperately needed a friend, but I confess I couldn't understand what Albert got out of it. He told me later I was like a flower growing in that rough place.

If the other boys—the toughs—came round and tried to pester me, he told them off. There would be an exchange of words and curses—never blows—but they always did go away.

Can I express how safe that made me feel?

We talked about our families—we'd both had one, once—and of the present. Rarely of the future. I found out his brother, Gerald, was bunged up in jail for thievery.

"Ma died when we was little. Pa brought us up. He always said Gerald would end at the gallows."

I must confess, I hung on every word Albert said. It was as if when he spoke to me the light in him flowed to me right along with those words.

"Do you think he will?"

"End at the gallows?" Albert shrugged. "Probably."

I should have known then how Albert came by his money, that he didn't run errands as I vaguely imagined or pick up work a day at a time. My innocence was fast fleeting, and I might have tumbled to it. Perhaps I didn't want to admit my hero took after his brother to such an extent.

"What will you do then?" Gerald was his last remaining relation in the world, for his Pa had passed some two years ago. I didn't want to imagine what I'd do without Ma.

"Keep on as I am, I suppose."

Albert did not often give me money. I expect he did not often have it to spare. But he kept the nasty lads away and made a great difference in my life.

Soon after Mr. Grimp's last visit, Ma came to me

with a desperate look in her eyes.

"That friend of yours," she asked, "does she know the other women hereabouts?" We kept much to ourselves. Ma didn't speak to the neighbors.

"He."

"Eh?"

"My friend is a *he*, not a she."

Ma stared at me and her frown deepened. "Polly, I hope you're not doing anything you shouldn't. I want you to stay a good girl."

"I'm not, Ma. He's just a friend."

"Nice?"

"Very nice."

She bit her lip. "I don't suppose you can ask him for the name of a local woman who knows—about babies and such."

I tumbled to the truth. "You're going to get rid of it."

"Yes."

My gaze fell to her belly. "But isn't that dangerous?"

"Everything's dangerous, Polly. I don't know where to turn."

A difficult thing for a child to hear a parent admit. But I'd known for some time she struggled. And now sheer desperation looked at me from her eyes.

No light, not any more. Ma had carried the light back when she and Pa used to laugh together, and it made everything feel right.

"I'll go find Albert. Ask," I told her.

"Tell him I have money. Mr. Grimp gave it to me."

"I'll try and find out. But I might not be able to locate Albert."

She wrapped her arms around her belly and sat on the edge of the bed. "Go. Try."

I did.

Chapter Five

I'd never before gone looking for Albert. He just turned up when I went out into the Close. Or he didn't. I knew not where among the tenements he lived. And when I went out now, I saw him nowhere in the yard.

I did see some of the lads with whom he frequently played games and argued. Big lads, older than me. I feared to approach them even just to ask after Albert.

Some women also stood in the yard, hanging half frozen laundry and queuing for the toilet. I decided they would be safer to approach than the boys.

I edged up to the nearest two women and addressed the first of them, a thin dame with a dirty cloth tied round her head,

"Excuse me, missus?"

She didn't hear me. I had to ask three times before she turned an annoyed visage in my direction.

"Wot is it?"

"Do you know a lad lives here called Albert Coward?"

"Might do. Why?"

"I need to speak with him."

"He stays over there." She gestured at the center block of the building. "But don't go inside."

"Why not?"

She cackled. Her companion, an older woman with iron-gray hair, cackled also.

"Pretty thing like you might not come out again."

I felt the danger inherent in her words. Danger of one sort or another, it seemed, lay everywhere in my world.

The woman went on, "I know who you belong to—that fancy piece up in the back."

Fancy piece? I wasn't sure what that meant.

As if to clarify her statement she added, "Mrs. High-and-Mighty, thinks she's better than everybody else."

That couldn't be Ma.

The woman with the gray hair spoke. "Seems this piece might belong to Albert Coward, duck." An arch note in her voice brought a flush to my cheek.

"Albert's a right one," the turbaned woman agreed. "Proper clever." Speaking to me, she said, "He's likely out and about now, doing his business."

"I need to speak with him."

"I'll just bet you do." They both laughed.

"If you see him, will you tell him so?"

"Sure thing, duck."

Not certain what else to do, I retreated to my corner. I could have asked the women for what Ma needed, but I wanted to protect her privacy and didn't think she'd want it all over the Close that she had Mr. Grimp's brat in her belly.

Sometime after noon, Albert came back. He glanced into my corner and came immediately to join me.

"Polly, wot you doing out here in the cold?"

No reason to tell him our room felt every bit as cold as the yard. "Waiting for you."

The light in his eyes brightened. I took it to mean

he was pleased. "Well, here I am."

Here I am. It was as if he offered himself to me. I let out a long breath of relief.

In a hushed voice I explained to him all about Ma's situation. I thought he might judge her then—judge us—but his expression never changed.

"Do you know of a woman who—who—" I faltered over what I did not completely understand.

"Here, in the Close?" he asked.

I shrugged.

"Might be better to bring somebody in from outside. I'll see what I can do."

"She can pay. Mr. Grimp gave her the coin."

"Right. She sure she wants to do this, though? I've heard of women dyin'."

I said, "If I try and talk her out of it, then we'll have a babe to look after. We haven't the room or enough food."

"Yeah, but—"

We stared into one another's eyes. The idea of Ma dying terrified me more than anything, though I knew it could happen. Pa had died, and Mary. Ma was all I had in the world except Albert.

"I know of a woman I can maybe ask," Albert said, "so long as you're sure."

So you see, it was my decision after all. And everything that followed can be laid at my feet.

****

The woman to whom Albert spoke—I never knew her name—sent another woman. That woman was called Mrs. Ruby, and an ordinary enough person she appeared, considering her business. She wore a neat brown dress and a trim bonnet, and had a plain, sensible face.

I let her into our room, and Ma rose to meet her. I saw, as Mrs. Ruby came in, she carried a case a little like a physician's bag.

"How you want to do this?" Mrs. Ruby asked Ma.

Ma fluttered her hands, and Mrs. Ruby looked at her belly.

"You look like you're pretty far along." She jerked her head at me. "This your daughter?"

"Yes. I want her out of it. Polly, go wait downstairs."

"Stay where you are, girl. Your ma will need your help. You have the money, missus?"

Ma nodded. "How much?"

"Thruppence."

Ma handed it over, enough to keep us for a week.

Mrs. Ruby tucked it into her bosom and gestured at her case. "I have instruments. Or a draught. Take your pick."

Ma paled. "I don't rightly know."

"Instruments are quicker and a sure job. The draught—sometimes it don't work, but usually it do."

"I—uh—" Ma's eyes rolled frantically. The light had never been farther from her. "What kind of instruments?"

Mrs. Ruby opened the case and showed Ma what lay inside. I couldn't see from where I stood. Ma backed up and sank down on the edge of the bed.

"Is—is it dangerous?"

"'Course it's dangerous. But I've done it hundreds of times."

"Ma," I reconsidered, "maybe we shouldn't—"

"You hush." Mrs. Ruby turned on me. "This is

your ma's choice."

Only it wasn't. It was the choice of Mr. Grimp and of the employers who wouldn't have an expectant mother to work for them, backed by the need to keep a roof over our heads.

I saw that so clearly then. I saw it in Ma's face before she spoke.

"Draught. I'll take the draught."

"You sure? I'll have to mix it up for you to drink and then leave you. Takes some time to work. I can't spend all night here."

"The draught."

Mrs. Ruby mixed it on our scrap of a table, and it smelled pungent enough to do all manner of harm.

"Drink the whole of it," she impressed upon Ma before she left. "And let it do its work."

Ma nodded.

After Mrs. Ruby left, Ma and I looked at each other.

"Do you trust her?" I asked. I wasn't sure I did. I trusted only two people in the world, Ma and Albert.

"I don't know. I've paid her the thruppence."

"What if it's poison?"

Ma shrugged. "I don't doubt it is. Meant to kill the sprog, innit?"

"What if it kills you?"

Ma repeated, "I've paid the thruppence." As if the turning of the world depended on spending three pennies.

I see now what a fool I was. I should have got Mrs. Ruby's direction—I did not. I merely let her walk out into the gathering night.

I should never have let Ma drink the draught. But I

stood there watching while she did, saw her gag as she forced it down.

Afterward she laid herself down on the bed and waited. We both waited.

For a long time nothing happened, except that Ma said the draught made her feel sick. She threw up, but not much. Later, she threw up a little bit again.

I went out to empty the pot in the toilet. In the short time I left her alone, everything changed.

I came back and found her writhing in agony, with pains to her belly that doubled her over around the bulk of the child. We'd got her into her nightgown beforehand, and she looked so frail. She had her long blonde hair braided and appeared little more than a girl, apart from her strained face.

I have witnessed many an awful thing since, but none matched the dreadful scene that followed. The two of us, with the door firmly closed, struggled alone while the pains tore through Ma's body.

I supposed the child would be born, expelled from her, but it didn't happen that way. Sometime in the small hours while she sweated and wept, I saw to my horror how she bled.

And bled, and bled.

What should I have done? She wanted so to keep it all a secret. Thrice I begged her to let me go for help—a physician or one of the women, since I did not know Mrs. Ruby's direction. Thrice she refused. I suppose I should have disobeyed her. It might have saved her life.

By the time dawn tinted the sky the bed lay awash with blood. The thick, heavy scent of it filled the room and clogged my throat.

Ma had grown weak and still. When I asked her

once more if I should go for help she did not answer. So I took up my coat and went out.

I met Albert just coming from his door. He took one look and ran to me.

"What is it, Polly?"

"Ma's dying. She's dying! We have to find Mrs. Ruby."

"Show me."

I took him up to that terrible room that stank of blood. We went in to find Ma staring sightlessly at the wall.

"Jesus," Albert breathed.

"We have to bring Mrs. Ruby. She has to save her."

"It's too late. Darlin', I'm sorry, it's too late. Jesus Christ. Darlin', she's dead."

"No. No, she's not. She can't be. Oh, what am I to do? What?" It came from me in a wail.

"Hush. Polly, hush." He took me in his arms and pressed my face against his chest.

"But she's gone," I grieved. "Gone! I have no one."

"You have me. I'll take care of you, see? I'll take care of you."

The words must have penetrated past my terror and pain. They allowed me to breathe again. I took only a short refuge in his arms before tearing free to look at the terrible scene on the bed. "I should have known," I whispered.

Albert spoke a particularly bad word followed by, "That damn woman killed her."

But he was wrong—I knew I had.

Chapter Six

Like my father and sister before her, Ma was wrapped in a sheet and carried to a pauper's grave. This time the sheet was bloody, but it was all I had to give her.

And that means we're all lying in paupers' graves now, we members of the Bridger family. For I lie here surrounded by all these silent others, none of us with so much as a penny.

A funny thing, that while living in the world money counts for so much, and lying here it means nothing at all. The things I did for money enough to buy a scrap of bread! Those of us here in the grave need not worry for such.

For certain, Ma had stopped worrying when they carried her out. It was all left to me.

I stood with Albert and some women from our building whom I didn't even know, while she left our room. The women—gawkers, Albert called them—surveyed the room and clucked their tongues.

"Plenty of scrubbing to do here," they said and left without offering to help.

I am not ashamed to admit I wept. Albert closed the door softly and once more took me in his arms.

"Now, Polly."

"What am I to do?"

"Stay here."

"How? Mr. Grimp will want paying. I won't, I won't—" I gulped.

"No, you won't. He will not lay a filthy finger on you. Look at me, Pol."

I did. I gazed into his eyes, seeking the light.

"I told you I'll take care of you."

"How?" I asked again. "The rent will need paying."

"Then you'll pay it. I'll pay it."

"How?" I squawked once more like a cawing crow. I knew he had but pennies in his pocket.

"I'll manage. You're my flower, understand? I'll do whatever it takes."

God help me, I had no real idea then just what that meant.

He went out, and I scrubbed that room the best I could. I had little hot water and only scraps of rag for cleaning cloths. But I swabbed up my mother's blood and wept all the while.

If I ever saw Mrs. Ruby again, I thought as I worked, I would kill her, though I didn't know how. She must have been aware of the agony to which she left Ma when she took her thruppence and left.

But no, I reminded myself as I choked on my tears. Ma's death was my fault, for I'd asked Albert to find a woman, and I'd stood by while Ma drank the poison.

I could have prevented it all.

The bloodstains remained when I was done. And when Mr. Grimp came by several days later, I pointed them out with a shaking finger.

"Look."

"Where's your mother, you foolish girl?"

Had he not heard? Hard to imagine, with the way

gossip traveled in the Close. No matter, for I told him. I suppose I anticipated an exclamation of horror. Instead he just shrugged.

"The brat died with her, I hope?"

I could not speak to answer him.

He fixed me with a muddy eye. "You have the rent?"

"No, not yet. I will." I believed in Albert. "You have to give me time."

"How old are you now?" His glance turned speculative.

"Twelve."

"You and I might come to an arrangement, if you don't want to be put out on the street."

"Get out," I whispered.

He ignored that. "It's unheard of for you to have this whole big place to yourself. A family could be livin' here. I have people asking."

Make him go away, I began to chant in my head, *make him go, make him go, make him—*

His small eyes prodded at me greedily. "You have to make it worth my while, keeping you here."

"I'll pay the rent."

"How?"

"I'll go out to work."

"Better you should do your work right here."

Make him go, make him—

"I might put the rent up."

"No, don't. Please." Despair touched my heart. I thought I'd tasted despair when Pa died, but it had been nothing like this.

He smiled. "You think about it, girl. You think why you'd better be nice to me. Next time I come I want the rent, or your favors."

I thought of him grunting over Ma on the bed and feared I'd vomit.

But at least my fervent prayers worked, for he went away then. And the next day, right around noon, Albert knocked on my door.

I hauled it open expecting the vile Grimp, only to see Albert with the light in his eyes. My relief must have been palpable.

Quickly he stepped in. "All right, Pol?"

I wasn't all right. On the other hand, I felt much better for his company.

I blurted, "I don't like it much here alone. It feels like there's something—somebody—in the room with me."

"You believe in ghosts?"

I never had. But then, I'd never been shut into a room along with someone's bloodstains and the raw memory of her agony. I shook my head and told him, "I need to go out to work. There must be some job I can do. I used to help Ma sew. Or there's the match factory."

"You don't want to go there." He raised his hand and touched my cheek. His fingers felt cold, and I wondered where he'd been.

"Mr. Grimp came last night asking for the rent."

"It's still two days till rent's due."

"Is it? He wants—" My throat closed.

"I know what he wants. Never mind." Albert dug in his pocket and pulled out a number of coins, which he counted carefully into my hand. My eyes widened as they followed his movements.

"Where did you get all that?"

"Does it matter? Should be enough for the rent, right?"

"Yes. But Albert, how?"

"Never you mind. Put that away safe. Keep your door locked when you're here. You might not like being shut in, but it's better than…just better, innit?"

I didn't know. He understood much more of the world than did I. "But if I could work—"

"Not now, not yet. If somewhat should happen to me, Pol—"

Our eyes met, and I went breathless. *No, no, no, no, no, no, no*! I could not lose another person I loved.

"Tell me nothing will happen to you, Albert."

He shrugged. "I'll do me best, but it's a rough old world, innit?"

I stood staring at the coins in my hand, wondering what he'd traded for them. For *me*. Emotion burgeoned in my heart—warm, wide, and powerful.

Please, I whispered in my mind, *not him*.

He glanced around the room. "Tomorrow I'll bring some coal. You warm enough for now?"

I nodded. These emotions should keep me so.

"You have anything to eat today, Pol?"

Another nod, this one a lie. I'd had water. I wanted little else.

"Then, when old Grimp comes back, you give him that, and we'll be set till next month. If you need my help, ask one of the boys in the yard—him called Danny Pete."

"Which one's he?"

"Small and dark, got a withered arm."

I nodded. I'd seen him.

"He'll get word to me. I'll be out earning most the

time, see?"

Earning for me. I wanted to say a hundred things then. I wanted to ask him why he should do such a thing, why take on a heavy responsibility not his own. But the light in his eyes, strong and steady, enfolded me, an answer in itself.

I whispered, "Thank you."

"Whatever old Grimp offers you, you don't give in to him, understand?"

"Yes. But, Albert, how do you get the money?"

Again, his eyes met mine. Again, he replied, "Does it matter?"

Maybe it did. But then again, given the state of my world, maybe I couldn't afford to let it matter.

Looking back from where I now lie, I can see how innocent I was then despite all I'd witnessed. Pa's death and Mary's. What Ma had to do, to keep us. She'd done what she did in order to shelter me. And though I understood that still more terrible things lay out in the world, I'd not experienced them.

Not yet.

Chapter Seven

For the next three and a half years, give or take, Albert looked after me. He supplied my every need, from rent to the food that went in my mouth and an occasional item of clothing. He even arranged for me to do a small amount of sewing there in the room for a woman he called Mrs. Wall. It was piece work and paid very little, but it helped me keep my self-respect.

During that time our relationship grew and deepened in ways I cannot hope to describe and perhaps do not fully understand even yet. Despite all he did for me, Albert always insisted I owed him nothing. And he never—not even once—asked for anything in return.

Those in the Close talked about us. Of course they did. Before a year passed they were calling me his kept piece, even though we were both still children. Women—and many of the men—would stare when I came and went. The women would put their heads together and whisper. The lads looked speculative.

But nothing of an illicit nature went on between us. No, I was not so naïve that I could fail to understand what they thought, not with the example of Ma and Mr. Grimp behind me.

Mr. Grimp spoke of it a time or two when he came to collect the rent, always with a disgruntled look on his face.

"That lad still keeping you?"

"Yes."

"Having his way with you?"

"No."

He didn't believe me. Nobody did, but it was true. If I had to define the relationship between me and Albert I would call it friendship. Deep friendship mixed generously with love. I relied on him and appreciated so much about him. His strength. His courage and how very steadfast he was. His honor—for yes, though even I could no longer mistake how he made his—our—living, he possessed honor unmatched in that place, in that world. I appreciated his company and the laughter he afforded me.

I loved his light. Of all the things Albert brought me during those years, that sustained me best. I needed it, craved and desired it. Just to be with him, to sit and talk or remain silent satisfied me on an unplumbed level and let me find ease.

He carried the light within him, and so carried me.

What could I do but love him? Will you believe me if I say we did little more than hold hands? Holding hands with Albert brought me bliss. When we went out from the Close—which we did sometimes for entertainment or if he had the free time—we always linked fingers. And it made me feel inexplicably safe.

That. Even though we lived our lives surrounded by risk. I've wondered since whether the need to provide for me drove Albert farther into the life he chose. If so, then I harmed him every bit as much as I harmed Ma when I gave her that poisoned draught to drink.

By my second year of living under Albert's protection, he'd earned a name in the Close, and a following. At sixteen years of age he headed a troop of others who folk called "Al's Lads." It did not take me long to discover what Al's Lads got up to when they left the Close.

I did not condemn Albert for it. There were not many ways to make a living in our world, and my welfare relied on his success at his illicit profession.

The fact that he had others thieving for him bothered me only because it seemed to intensify our risk. People in the Close knew what he was about. Could discovery by the authorities fail to follow?

I knew full well that his beloved older brother still languished in prison. Sometimes—rarely enough—Albert went off to see him. He would come home grave-faced and with the light in his eyes terribly dimmed.

I tried to discuss the situation with him once or twice. Albert always heard me out quite patiently, when I spoke to him. It was no different now.

I well remember the first occasion I brought it up. Winter had come again. We sat side by side in my room near the fire for which he'd just brought in a measure of coal. He looked red from the cold and rubbed his hands together in an effort to warm them.

"Where have you been today?" I asked.

He laughed. "Where haven't I been? All round London. To the West End, even."

"With your troop of boys?"

He looked at me. It was the first time I'd mentioned the operation he ran, and he looked surprised. "How d'you know about that?"

"People talk. It sounds dangerous."

He shrugged. "Life's dangerous, Pol. You know it

as well as I do."

"What if you get caught?"

"Won't happen. I don't do the pinching meself anymore, see? At least not much."

"What if one of your boys gets taken in and talks?"

Albert shrugged again.

"What if the coppers take you? What will happen to me?"

He did not say the things he should—that he only floated the risk for my sake. He did not ask why my first concern would not be for *him*, in jail.

Instead he put his arm around me and pulled me close. "It won't happen."

"It might. Albert, I couldn't survive without you." I didn't mean just the rent or the food he bought. The sense of protection he provided. But if his light disappeared from my world, I could see only darkness ahead.

"Why borrow worry?" he asked.

"I don't borrow it. It's always following me."

"Why hold up and let it catch you, then? Just keep walking."

"I can't help it. I can't."

That was the first time he kissed me on the lips. Oh, there'd been smooches on the cheek before, given in reassurance or affection. And that was how it started now, with him kissing away the tears on my cheeks before he brushed his lips across mine.

I went silent with astonishment. When he kissed me, I could *taste* his light.

"Here, Pol, rest your head." He drew it against his shoulder and I closed my eyes, and the fear—at least most of it—flowed away.

Always was it so, between us.

After a while he said, "Pol, I'll always be here for you. And if I should have to go away for a while—should I get bunged up, say—I promise I'll always return to you. Right?"

"Right."

"You believe me?"

I believed him. But I had no idea, then, what might come between us.

****

As time passed Albert spent more and more time with me there in my room. At some point he lost his place in his old quarters or perhaps gave it up to someone else. And he would sleep in my room, but we never did anything more—so I swear—than cuddle and kiss. We might even share the same bed, the one where Ma had died, and I confess I liked that best. But none of what folk said about us was true.

He spent many nights out on what he called the game. He tried never to bring that back to the room or to involve me. But sometimes one of the lads would run up the narrow stairs to find him. And I heard bits and pieces of things when we were out in the yard.

The lads treated him with respect. So, for the most part, did others in the Close. I never saw him speak harshly or behave cruelly toward anyone. But he never behaved as gently with anyone as with me.

Queen Pol, the folk in the Close began to call me. *She never gets her hands dirty.*

But I did. I scrubbed our little room—for I could no longer deny it was *ours*—and our clothing, Albert's as well as mine. I continued with the piece work, sewing until my eyes crossed. I stretched what money

Albert brought to make it serve.

When Mr. Grimp came to collect the rent, I could hear his progress all up and down the building. Women shrieked and children wailed. Nobody ever had the coin to pay in full.

Except me.

However he accomplished the feat, Albert always assured I had the coin in hand when Grimp showed up at the door. The landlord never made an advance or said an inappropriate word to me. Instead he'd look at the floor, take his rent and leave.

I wondered what Albert had to do to get that money. That is, I knew—roughly—but could only imagine what it took. In lean months there might be barely enough. He would give it to me and say, "There you go, Pol. Don't spend it on anything else, right? No food for now. I'll buy food when I can. Rent always comes first, hear?"

Rent always came first.

I see now, from this peaceful place where I lie, how sheltered I was. Trouble did come into the Close— sickness and violence and sometimes the coppers. At such times people there banded together. But I never felt a true part of them, a fact borne out later.

I must have been fifteen or so, and Albert all of seventeen the first time he spoke his intentions out to me. I remember well it was summer—a summer evening—and very warm. The entire yard reeked of the toilets, and fever ran through the tenements.

The coppers had also been creeping round, and Albert was home that night, lying low. I remember we lay in the bed side by side, him with his shirt off and me in just my shift, holding hands.

I felt too warm to sleep. There was no air. I lay listening to the sounds of the Close—babes wailing and people arguing. A loud fight across the way. I wondered if this was all I'd ever know.

"Albert?" I whispered.

"Yes, Pol?"

"What's going to happen to us?"

"What d'you mean?"

I moved restlessly. Albert, a great believer in getting on, tended to put one foot in front of the other. But on this stifling night I needed something more.

"What does our future hold?"

He reached up and touched my face. No one before or since has ever touched me the way Albert did. I swear, even in the dark I could feel his light.

As always he seemed to know what I needed—in this case, reassurance.

"We'll be together of course. Like this."

"Like this?"

"Only better. I mean to marry you, Polly, when you're old enough."

A thrill went through me from head to toe.

"Marry?"

"I've never wanted anything else from the first. I knew then, Pol, you were the girl I meant to marry."

"When will I be old enough?"

"Dunno. Soon."

"People in the Close talk about us. They think we—"

"I know what they think. But we two know the truth, eh?"

"Will we live here always? Even after we— marry?" I whispered the last word.

"I dunno that either. I'd like something better, but it's a steep hill to climb. I tell you, Pol, I've been climbing. But it's a tough go."

"No matter." My hand cradled his. At that moment I had everything I needed.

"Polly…" He turned toward me in the bed. I could barely see him, just an outline in dirty silver, like tarnish. "Polly, I love you. I want you to know that, to hold it close if ever—well, if ever anything happens."

"I love you too, Albert."

"Do you?"

"My heart…" I fumbled for the words. "My heart is yours."

"Then we're as good as married already, ain't we?"

We were, then and forever.

Chapter Eight

Everyone should be loved the way Albert and I loved each other, at least once in his or her life. Each of us should know the comfort of the unbreakable bond that forms, the deep trust, and the gift of believing somebody holds us above all others for whatever reason. For I did not understand—do not understand yet—why Albert so valued me. I should have sworn it was because he thought me pretty, but what came after disproved that.

I am pretty no longer. Laid here with others of my kind, I know that for the truth. So Albert must in fact have loved something else about me.

He was eighteen and I nearly sixteen when disaster struck. Late autumn had once more come to the Close. The wind that blew around the bricks and cobbles grew colder. I tried to prepare in body and spirit for the winter ahead.

Life proved difficult at all times in the Close, and in winter doubly so. Albert brought me a fine coat— stolen from heaven knows where—and some warm hose. He was away much just then, and when we were together he seemed tense. I thought he just felt the compulsion to store up funds against the season, for he gave me extra coins here and there and told me not to spend them.

"Not yet, Pol. You keep those, see? Against what

might come."

I remember one time in particular he came to me as I sat by the fire and put the pennies in my hand. And I gazed long into his eyes. The light there, that which allowed me to live, seemed to have dimmed.

"What's to happen?" I asked, my old apprehension returning.

"You never know." He hesitated. "You have the rent for December?"

"Yes."

"Then you can set old Grimp right when he comes."

"Albert, what's amiss?"

He sat down beside me. "Pol, two of the lads got taken. I don't think they'll talk. They're all loyal to me. But if they do, see, I might be for it. I'm the ringleader. And that's who the coppers want to nab."

I stared at him, appalled. Though I'd long known how he made his living—our living—he'd never said it out so plain. Terror made me say, "You—get taken? To jail, you mean?"

He did not answer.

And I asked cravenly, selfishly, even as I had once before, "What will happen to me?"

"You'll be all right if I go down for a while." He nodded at the pennies in my hand. "You'll have a bit put by."

My terror, I discovered, knew no reason. I'd lost Pa and Ma. I could not lose Albert.

This was not the future I wanted to see. Marriage, a life spent with him in safety—not more darkness.

Yet I lie here in darkness now, do I not? And it's not as terrible as what came before.

"Pol, don't look like that. I'm hoping it won't happen. Or I'll be able to talk my way out of it, if it does. You'll sit tight, see? Wait for me."

"Oh, Albert—"

"I'll always come back to you. Always. Understand?"

Just like that, his warmth enfolded me. He reached out and took me in his arms and kissed me as if he wanted to drink my fear and take it away.

Many things have been said about Albert Coward, then and since. Thief, blackguard. No better than he should be. But I swear I could feel his goodness then, that night. It underlay all the things he did and the way he was forced to live, like his bones beneath the flesh.

As always, his touch calmed me. But beneath the surface my fear remained.

****

After that, Albert said little to me about any arrests. Even when I asked him he merely shrugged and put me off. But he remained tense and watchful.

Three days before my birthday it was, at the end of November, when Charlie came to me. Charlie, one of Albert's runners, was perhaps my age, thin as a bundle of sticks, with a sharp, cunning face.

"Miss Polly," he said.

They all called me that, did Albert's boys. I had not much beyond casual contact with them. But now I came out into the late afternoon light to empty my pot into the toilet. Far better, I'd decided, than using that malodorous facility. Charlie broke away from a wad of other lads and hurried to me.

I remember the day was wet and chilly. Already, the dark of evening fell and hard bits of sleet struck my cheek, driven by a bitter wind.

I paused when Charlie reached me and dread rose up, a wave so powerful I knew all before the lad spoke.

"He's been taken, Al has. He wanted me to bring word to you."

"Taken." My lips felt frozen.

"By the coppers. Not two hours ago."

My knees wobbled beneath me. I set the pot down so I wouldn't drop it. "Where? Where did they take him?"

"Newgate, for now. He'll go up before the magistrates."

"No," I moaned. The need that arose inside me felt monstrous, stronger even than the fear and dread. I needed Albert to come walking back down the alley into the Close, needed him to smile and tell me it had all been a misunderstanding. I needed the feel of his fingers on mine.

"How long?" I asked. "How long before he comes home?"

"Devil knows. I sure don't." Charlie eyed me. "You all right, miss?"

I most definitely was not all right. But they all stared now—the others of Albert's boys and the folks who lived in the Close and knew who I was. I had my pride. So I nodded.

"Thank you for telling me. Will you bring me any news?"

"Sure, miss."

I emptied the pot and went back inside, all while they continued watching me. I sat in front of my meager fire, too stricken to cry.

I had almost no coal for the fire. I'd hoped Albert

might bring me more today. He would not, now. I had some food in the house, but it wouldn't last long.

All of that paled, though, in comparison with his absence. Given, Albert was away a lot. But the promise of his return remained always with me—the certainty that he'd be with me sooner or later and restore completeness to my life. This—this felt like losing an arm or leg.

Indeed, I am not sure I'd understood what Albert meant to me till that moment. Oh, I'd appreciated him, I had. Even feared this loss. But the emptiness that now engulfed me taught me some things about myself and him.

My thoughts were not all selfish. I ached for Albert, I did, and wondered what befell him that night. I'd heard tales of Newgate—we all had—and could not bear to think of him there. I wanted him home with me, for this room seemed a palace by comparison.

He'll come in the morning, I assured myself. They'll release him and he'll hurry home, just as he promised, back to me.

But the morning brought only more chilly wind, a rime of ice on the cobbles in the yard, and no answers. I went out with my good, new coat wrapped around me and stood at the end of the alley watching for him.

Any number of people passed by. Even so early, they thronged the street beyond the alley, but none had a tinge of red in his hair and a confident stride, or smiling gray eyes that saw only me.

I stood there a long time, till my toes and fingers grew numb. Then I told myself, *He'll come at noontime. Silly chit, the magistrates won't be doing business so early as this.*

I went back inside and waited.

People do not escape the walls of Newgate easily and news only slightly more so. Three interminable days passed before we got word of any kind. My coal and food both ran out. I ventured beyond the Close to buy food, even though Albert had told me not to spend any of the coin.

Once out there, I took a madness in my head. I walked all the way to Newgate. A formidable edifice it did present with coppers out front and any number of other passersby, some arguing with the officers stationed at the door.

As I stood there watching, wondering what befell Albert—my Albert—in such a place, the sun came out.

And I could feel his light. It seemed as if, though trapped inside with him, it nevertheless flowed out to embrace me, the way his arms might.

I stood there shivering in the bright sunshine—such a rarity in London—with tears streaming down my face. And I tried to pray.

Ma had taught me my prayers when I was young, to be said when she tucked me into my cot at night. But all the words had been replaced with longing. I wanted to see Albert come striding out the door. My entire body and all my spirit demanded it.

I still possess a body, lying here in this grave. As I've said, I can feel it yet in a distant way, like a limb gone asleep.

I must have a spirit also. Else who is it thinking these thoughts, who telling this tale of how I came to fall so low in the world?

And of he who, even apart from me, remained my strength.

Chapter Nine

Three more days would pass before I needed to pay
the rent. The whole Close talked about me then,
perhaps speculating what I would do now my protector
had gone.

The women eyed me. So did the lads—those Albert
had kept at bay—but with a different kind of
speculation. I might have expected Albert's lads to
band together and protect me, but they did not. I hoped
Albert's reputation might keep trouble from my door,
but that did not happen either.

The women of the Close considered me snooty
because I kept to myself. I did so out of fear, only. I
certainly never considered myself better than them.

I walked down to Newgate daily and stood there in
my good coat that felt so like Albert's arms wrapped
around me, watching the place.

Once, while I was away, someone broke into my
room. I came home to find the door jimmied open and
my belongings scattered. Not that I had much. The thief
no doubt hoped to find money there but I am—was—
not entirely green, and I had every penny Albert had
given me secreted about my person.

Still, even though I'd lost little, it felt a blow. A
few of my dishes and the wash basin had been broken.
A blanket was gone.

Oh, how I ached for Albert then! I wanted him to

come walking down from Newgate—miraculously freed-—and take to task those who'd acted against me. I wept in my lonely bed that night.

When Mr. Grimp came the next day, though, I was able to pay him the rent. He stood there in the doorway and regarded me from his cruel, tiny eyes while I counted the coins into his hand.

When I finished, he said, "I hears your young man's got himself bunged up. What you going to do now, eh?"

I declared, "Albert will be back soon."

"Maybe. Maybe not. How old are you now, Polly Bridger?"

"Sixteen."

"Plenty old enough."

I did not ask for what. I knew. I shrank away from him and began to shut the door.

"I'll be back, Polly Bridger. I'll be back next month."

****

You might measure a month as a long while. And it can be when you have no food, when you're cold or suffering some terrible sickness. But I will tell you, it can also pass very swiftly when one is caught in a situation such as mine.

With the rent paid I had very little left to me, just the few extra pennies Albert had brought and those I'd earned sewing, which he'd bidden me keep. It went for food. I had no extra for coal and so shivered in that room as the winter exhaled its icy breath into Bishop's Close. Nights were the worst when I lay in the bed, wearing every stitch of clothing I owned and shivered. The walls sweated damp, and it rained so many days in a row I lost count. Everybody in the Close had a cough, and I sniffled right along with them.

I would have been pleased to continue with my stitching for the one or two pennies it earned me. But I did not know how to reach Mrs. Wall. Albert had always brought the pieces to me and had not shared my employer's full name or her direction.

Even had I possessed friends in the Close there was no charity to be found. Most were as bad off as me, some worse. Mr. Grimp threw two families out because they couldn't pay their rent. A baby died, and an old woman.

I saw her carried out all wrapped in a grubby sheet, her form looking too small to be a full-grown person. Talk in the yard said she'd starved to death, having lost her family.

I did not want to starve to death, so I went out looking for work. I'd been venturing out to Newgate, so the world beyond the Close did not seem so frightening. In truth I'd had no real taste of the world but felt emboldened enough to seek for a wage.

I want you to know I did not sit in that room and wait to die, like that old woman. Nor by then did I expect anyone to rescue me—though I will admit I still longed for it.

I had some notion I might go out and find a position sewing, that being my only skill. Failing that, I might be trusted to run errands or work in a shop for pennies, enough to let me eat and perhaps put something aside toward January's rent, which loomed hideously over my head.

The biggest flaw in my thinking was that no one in East London could afford to hire anyone else, and if I stepped beyond those borders no one was willing to trust me. Looking as I did—ragged beneath the good coat Albert had given me—those who could pay regarded me with nothing but suspicion.

I remember going into one shop not far from the prison, inquiring for work. An old woman, stooped and bent, ran the place. I figured she could use some help. I even fancied I might throw myself on her mercy.

"Wot you want?" she barked, eyeing me up and down.

"Work," I told her as I did in all such cases. "I hoped you'd take me on."

She snorted. "No work here."

"There must be." I examined the shelves, only thinly stocked. It looked a grim place. "I could reach things off the high shelves for you and run errands. A penny a week?"

Her cold eyes raked me again and I saw no charity in them. "You want to take the bread from my mouth?"

"No, missus, just to put a bit in mine."

Her next question fair knocked me back on my heels. "You want to sell that coat?"

"Eh?"

"Sell your coat, if you want to eat. I'll give you tuppence."

I wrapped my arms around my body defensively. Albert's coat was all that kept me warm, and I wore it day and night.

"But it's cold out."

She shrugged. It seemed at that moment her indifference defined my life. No one cared if I ate or froze to death. No one cared if I lived or died.

But Albert cared, and he would return to me. I had

only to keep myself—somehow—till he arrived.

I love you, Polly.

"I can't sell my coat. Do you know anywhere else I might get work?"

"Try the match factory."

I'd been avoiding that. I remembered all too well what Ma had said of the girls who worked there, and Albert had also warned me about the place. I'd continued seeing some of those workers since in the streets—many with their faces covered.

But needs must, and the next morning I walked to the factory and asked for work.

I got an eyeful of what those women looked like then. Indeed, I did. And I shuddered at the thought of joining their ranks, of ever looking like them, though in truth I came to look much worse later on. But I went in and I asked of person after person, seeking the manager.

One of the girls I asked laid her fingers on my arm. "You don't want to work here, duck."

I looked into her eyes and saw—kindness. Blue eyes they were, not unlike Ma's, and what I could see of her looked pretty. But she had one of those cloths wrapped around the bottom of her face.

"Betty," one of the other women said to her, a caution.

The woman with the blue eyes said, "She thinks she wants to work here." She withdrew her fingers from my arm and unwrapped the cloth from her face.

Oh, what I saw! To be sure, I've seen worse since. Or maybe not. She had a hole straight into the side of her face. Through it, I glimpsed her gums and teeth.

Hastily she retied the cloth to cover the hole, while

I fought down sickness. Good thing I'd had nothing to eat that day.

I dragged my gaze back to her eyes and there saw something else—a dim flicker of light like that Ma had, once—like the light Albert carried.

Despite everything.

"You don't want to work here," she repeated. "What's in them vats causes this."

"But I'm starving," I confessed.

She dug in her pocket and came up with a penny. The other women all hooted and exclaimed in protest.

A man approached. He wore a gray suit with a check in the fabric and looked well-fed. He scowled at me.

"What's all this? The lot of you, get to work." The women scurried off, and the gentleman bent a hard gaze on me.

"What are you doing here?"

"I need a job." There was the truth of it. I needed a job—I certainly did not want one, there.

"Get off," he told me rudely.

"But—"

"We are not hiring."

"Sir, I am desperate for work." I licked my lips. "I need to be able to pay next month's rent."

"Come back later. If someone leaves, or if someone dies, there might be an opening."

If someone dies.

I thought of Betty with the light banked in her eyes. My own eyes filled with tears.

"Clear off," he ordered. And thinking he'd never hire me later if I argued with him now, I went.

Cold fog filled the streets and blurred everything

before my eyes.
Or maybe that was the tears.
I ached for Betty.
I ached for the light.

Chapter Ten

"Al's been sent down, he has. Three years."

Charlie delivered the news to me as soon as I set foot out the door next morning, bent on emptying the chamber pot. My heart fell so violently, I swayed on my feet.

Nearly a month had passed since Albert's arrest. Christmas—the worst I'd known since Ma died—had come and gone. Betty's charity had long since been spent on bread, and my stomach once more felt so hollow it hurt.

The rent would be due in three days.

Others of Al's boys stood in the yard watching as Charlie gave me the word. Neighbors also populated the yard. A general air of gloom prevailed.

"Three years," I breathed. An eternity.

"For thieving."

"Where? Where is he?"

"Appeared before the magistrates yesterday afternoon. Was sentenced, wasn't he? Might stay in Newgate or be sent farther afield."

"I want to go and see him." I'd been outside Newgate enough times, never within.

Charlie examined me with cautious blue eyes. "He wouldn't want you there, miss."

"I don't care."

"Best to wait and see if he gets moved."

Wait. It seemed to be all I ever did. I wanted so desperately to see Albert, to gaze into his eyes. Maybe then I could endure what must come.

But could I? Mr. Grimp. The factory. Or starvation. *I'll come back to you, Polly.*

"Charlie, I don't have enough money for the rent." Or to eat, but that was secondary. "Do you know anybody would take me in?"

"You?" He snorted. "No."

"Why not?"

"Why should they? Can you pay your share?"

I shook my head.

A wise expression filled his homely face. "My ma used to say before she died, we ain't got room for charity."

He walked away. I stood there swaying as from a mighty blow, the pot still in my hands, the focus of far too many eyes. I forced myself into motion, emptied the pot and went up to my cold room.

There, I counted my pennies. Two. I would have wept, but my eyes seemed to have run dry. I might have prayed, but I had no words for any God who could have created my world.

What were my choices? Give in to what the vile Mr. Grimp would ask, for I knew he'd just been awaiting his opportunity to pressure me. Leave and starve on the streets. The streets had become a mighty specter in my life, one that had frightened me even when Ma was still alive.

I thought of what Ma had traded to keep us from the streets. I thought of how she'd died.

I wondered how Albert fared, if he were frightened—Albert did not scare readily, but I imagined such a fate as he faced might daunt anyone. I wondered if—and how—he kept well. Disease ran rampant in the prisons. He was young and strong, yes, but even such could be brought down.

Three years.

Three years, before I would touch his hand or feel him hold me in his arms. I wondered if he worried for me—I knew he did.

I had been fortunate so far, having other people to worry for me—Pa, Ma, and Albert. Now, most terrifyingly of all, I had no one to rely upon but myself.

****

Sometimes, so I have learned, events seem as inevitable as a cask rolling down a hill. Nothing can stop them. Perhaps me ending here in this grave was inevitable, like that. God himself could not have prevented it even had He wished.

He did not.

The progression of time is like that—you can no more stop it than halt the river from flowing. Time's a funny thing. People have chopped life up into days and years, hours and minutes, and caused the bells to ring out across the city just so they can pass.

The next three days passed. I did not want them to—even though I would have caused the next three years to pass if I could—but they did. Late in the afternoon of the last day of the year, Mr. Grimp knocked at my door.

He had another man at his back, a big burly man wearing a tattered top hat, who carried a cudgel and who served as Mr. Grimp's enforcer. Just think what a fat prize old Grimp would be as he progressed around collecting his rents. But the thug prevented anyone from bothering him.

"You have the rent?" Grimp asked.

Was that an avid gleam I saw in his eyes? He must have heard about Albert's fate. He knew I did not have the money. He looked forward to what must come next.

I ran my damp palms down the skirt of my dress and shook my head. "Not yet. I will have."

"When?"

Three years. But I couldn't possibly tell him that.

"I've got a chance of a job."

"Where?"

"The match factory." The man had told me to come back and see if there were any openings. I meant to go there first thing and beg for a place if I had to. Though it seemed wrong to hope someone like Betty had left a vacancy.

"So," I hurried on, "you see I'll be able to pay. Soon."

"Soon." He repeated the word like an epithet. He glanced at the man at his back and said, "Wait here." He stepped into my room and shut the door.

"Look, girl, this ain't a charity."

How many times had I heard those words?

"You know how valuable a big place like this is?"

This bit of a room? Ma and I together had barely been able to turn around. I thought of the musty air, the chimney that refused to draw up the poisonous smoke, the walls running with damp.

"I have whole families I could place here. Why should you have all this to yourself?"

My lips went stiff. "Put me somewhere else then. For less rent."

"I might. Or we could come to an arrangement like

I had with your mother."

Not that, no, not that, not—

The litany sang in my head.

"I've told you this before. It's simple. You pay me one way or you pay t'other."

Yes, he had told me before. That did not make it any more palatable.

"You want me to be kind to you, Polly Bridger? You be kind to me."

Kind? Like he'd been to Ma, forcing her to get rid of his child? I said, "What Ma did for you killed her."

He shrugged. "It's a hard world, girl. People die every day. It's the keeping out o' the grave that matters, right?"

I said naught. I might do many things to keep out of the grave. But lying down with Mr. Grimp was not one of them.

To my immense relief he swung the door back open so the man outside could hear. "Listen, girl, because it's the holiday season and I'm feeling generous, I'll give you some time."

"Time? How much?" *Another month. Let him say another month.*

"Three days."

"I—I might be able to give you part o' the rent by then. Would that be enough?"

"Three days, and I'll want all of it paying or else your answer. Hear?"

I heard. So that was his notion of generosity. Coercion, more like. He wanted what he wanted of me and no excuses. I will admit the future looked dark after he left, even more than it usually did. I could see barely a glimmer of light.

Chapter Eleven

The factory was closed next day, it being the holiday. But I took myself there early the morning after, determined not to come away without a place.

I remember the fog had moved in overnight, thick and chilly as a dead man's hand. It made ghostly the forms of the girls and women hurrying inside. They looked like wraiths escaped from hell.

That the match factory represented a hell, I did not doubt. But it frightened me less than did Mr. Grimp.

Single-minded, I ignored the staring eyes and determinedly sought out the man I'd seen before.

As soon as he laid eyes on me, he shook his head. "No jobs."

"Please." I clenched my fingers inside the long sleeves of my coat. "I'll do anything. Sweep the floor, run errands. I cannot pay my rent."

"Have you no family?"

"Dead. And—and my husband's had to go away." *Three years.*

"You're young to have a husband."

But such Albert was to me. And it had become clear I must do my part to keep alive till he could make good on his promise and return.

"Please," I said again, begging.

He seemed to consider it. Then he shook his head once more and pronounced shrewdly, "You do not look used to this kind of employment. And the work here is hard and dangerous."

He was right. I'd been working since a child with Pa and Ma, but not hard work. Yet despite the risks, I needed this.

"I'm quick. I'll pick most anything up."

"I think not."

"Sir"—I made so bold as to seize his sleeve—"I'll be out on the streets."

"Get off me." He drew away. As Betty had before him, he dug in his pocket and produced a penny which he gave to me. "Buy yourself something to eat, girl. And don't come back."

I spent the penny on bread. I could have got a nice fresh loaf from the baker's cart. It smelled like heaven. But he offered me a loaf and a half of stale bread which I knew would last longer. I returned with it to my room.

It had been days since I had a proper meal or much more than water. When I ate, it made me feel sick, and I almost lost what went down.

I huddled in the bed beneath my blanket in an effort to get warm and tried to think what I should do. I wondered if I might persuade Mr. Grimp to give me a bit more time when he returned. I doubted it.

He had me where he wanted me now. He'd waited like a big old spider hanging in a web, and I was caught.

I spent the rest of that day and the two that followed deciding what was worse—Grimp or the streets. I went out again looking for work—any work—and stole a shriveled apple from a cart because I was so hungry.

Seldom did I steal anything, though I'd lived off

that trade long enough. But that time would not be the last.

I ask you now, from my place lying here in this peaceful quiet, what should I have done? There was no charity available for the likes of me. And there were thousands of others just like me in the city.

Cast off like the trash in the gutters.

At least, I reminded myself, I was loved. I might not know where Albert was other than some terrible place he should not be. But he loved me still. I held that fact to me, so I did.

When Mr. Grimp returned, it was evening. He'd left me all that third day to hope—or worry. Perhaps he thought, given the position in which I found myself, I would just bid him come in and take his equivalent in rent that very night.

He came without his bodyguard and with a confident look in his tiny eyes.

"Well, girl? You have the rent?"

"No, sir."

"Then are you ready to deal with me?"

Deal with him. Was that what he called it? I remembered him grunting over Ma, and her bleeding to death.

I shook my head.

"Then you'll have to get out."

I knew. I knew that.

With what poise I could muster, I asked, "Could you not give me just a bit more time?"

"To what purpose? Have you a job?"

"No, sir."

"Have you another protector?"

I thought of Albert. What if, miraculously, he came

walking into the Close, up the stairs behind Mr. Grimp, and back into my life? What if he took me in his arms? Oh, I ached for it.

But there were no miracles for the likes of me.

"No, sir."

"Accommodate me this night, and I'll let you stay."

Well, there it was, plain and simple. I held my breath. So did Grimp.

"No, sir."

Anger filled him then. I felt it rise. I thought he might strike me down, but he didn't. "Then clear out."

"Sir?"

"You heard me."

"Tonight? But it's dark out." You must understand, I never ventured out alone after dark.

He laughed harshly. "Get your things and go. Don't come back. There'll be another family in here tomorrow."

Don't come back. It seemed to be what folk said to me.

I wanted to beg. I wanted to throw myself on his mercy. Some remaining shreds of dignity prevented it. Besides, I did not believe he possessed any mercy.

He stood watching while I gathered up my things, as if he thought I might steal something. There was nothing to steal. Had there been, I'd have sold it by now. In truth I had few possessions. An extra pair of hose. My blanket, my coat which I already wore.

I suppose Mr. Grimp expected I'd panic and give in to him at the end. I didn't. With a glance for Ma's bloodstains which still marked the floor, I went. I never returned there again.

****

For the first few nights, with nowhere to go, I walked the streets. I did not stray far from the Close, and it occurred to me I might go back there and hide in the yard—home is home, however wretched.

To my surprise, I found the streets were filled with others like me. After the dark came down, it was as if a curtain rose. The daytime people retired to their firesides, and the wraiths came out.

I thought of them as wraiths because they could be but dimly seen. The dark half-hid them, as did the fog. They were not always silent. Some sang drunken songs. Some cried out. Some struck their companions—I heard the blows.

Things sounded far different at night. The fog dampened ordinary voices and made them into frightening things, like the wails of demons. I cannot begin to describe how frightened I was. I crept about the very edges of the edges, as it were, and hoped no one would notice me. At night I wore my blanket. By day I begged for work and stole food to live.

By the third night I was so exhausted I fell asleep in the doorway of a shop. Recessed, it offered what to me felt like a measure of shelter. I slept but fitfully, wrapped in my coat and my blanket against the sharp chill.

I will tell you a funny thing about human nature. I awoke in that doorway at first light the next morning, and it felt like mine, my place, my bit of home. I returned to it four times and had just begun to feel safe there when the shopkeeper arrived early one morning and discovered me.

He roused me with a kick. "What are you doing

here? Be off."

I scrambled up and eyed him blearily. "Please, sir, I'm not hurting anything."

"Are you not?"

"I have nowhere else to sleep."

"Why choose my doorway?"

Wondering if he had any pity, I said, "It was raining. I had nowhere else."

"Clear off."

"Please—"

"You think I want my customers stumbling over a stinking pile of rags?"

Stinking pile of rags? Me?

I cleared off. And I wandered.

Chapter Twelve

Lying here now in this grave with so many others, with a stranger's chest beneath my shoulder, someone's arm slung across my ankle, all that happened next seems impossibly distant from me. For as I say, it's quiet here, but in my life then, there was no quiet to be found. No rest, no ease.

Home, however humble, is a place of ease. It seems I always knew that, deep down. Perhaps Pa taught it to me with his efforts to keep us safe under our roof. Ma taught it to me with her sacrifices, and Albert, dropping pence for the rent into my hand.

Once out on the streets, though, it all slipped away from me, and with it a measure of reality. I had no place to be. As a consequence, I had no one to be.

I asked everywhere I went for a job. I told them I could sew, but no one believed me. After but a week on the streets I looked so ragged and dirty no one would even consider dealing with me.

Well, one brand of person would.

The first time I was propositioned I did not understand what the gentleman meant. I'd taken to begging by then—I'd seen passersby toss the occasional coin at a waif. But I was too old, or so I found, to win much pity.

When the shabby hansom cab drew up beside me, I stuck out my hand. Those who lived here in these streets had no more to give than I. Those who passed through and could afford a carriage might offer better. The window in the cab door rolled down. A man leaned out.

"How much?"

For a dizzying moment, I supposed he asked the amount of charity I wished. The winter's day had just grown dark, and I could not see him well, but he might be an angel.

I quavered, "A penny?"

"You'll do it for a penny? Get in."

The cab door opened. To be more precise, it yawned open upon a blackness like that of hell. My instincts still operated, and I backed away.

"Quickly, girl, if you want paying."

I peered into his eyes. I ran. I cut down an alley and squeezed between two buildings as if the devil himself pursued me. I fetched up among some dust bins and spent the night there, huddled like a rat, terrified the man would find me.

It happened again and again, not always in that same way—not always out of a cab—but you understand what I mean. Each time I ran, no matter how hungry I was, telling myself, *Not that, no, not that.*

That winter proved a cold one. When it did not rain it sleeted, and when it did not sleet, it snowed. The fog became a presence, one that might be friend or foe. It served to hide me, for I was in constant danger. It also wrapped me in an icy blanket while I slept. Most times I could not feel my fingers or toes.

I survived by moving all the time, by stealing food, and by begging. Once, when I asked a gentleman for charity, he directed me to the workhouse.

"They'll feed you there," he said, staring down his nose at me, "and give you a bed."

I have to admit, I felt cold enough and tired enough to consider it. But Albert had spoken to me of such places and of what went on there.

"Folk go there when they're sick," he'd said, "or fixing to die."

I was not sick—not then—nor did I want to die. And before I could grow quite desperate enough to apply for succor there, I met Darcy.

This is how our meeting came about, that which would alter my life. Indeed, I'd no idea at the time what her significance to me would be. I'd been busy avoiding people, for the most part, and had lost track of the days. I had no idea how long I'd survived on my own. Surely no more than two weeks.

At length, exhaustion caught up with me. Exhaustion and hunger. The only time my stomach didn't hurt from being empty was when I slept, but I feared getting caught sleeping anywhere for long.

Under cover of the fog, I found a place on a doorstep in a narrow, fetid alley where I curled up in my blanket.

I remembered no more till a voice called repeatedly, "Here, here!"

I came to myself with a violent start. Wisps of fog floated down the alley like disembodied fingers. A figure stood over me, black against the paler darkness.

"Wot you doin' here?"

The voice belonged to a female, which reassured me only marginally. Both back in the Close and on the streets I'd seen enraged women do terrible things to one another.

I tried to scramble up, tripped on my blanket and tumbled down again.

"Wot's yer name?"

Not wanting to say, yet loathe to antagonize her, I asked, "Is this your place?" Early on I'd learned most safe spots were taken and would be defended.

"As a matter of fact, it is."

"I'm sorry. I didn't know."

She shifted her weight and looked at me. I couldn't tell how much she could see—there wasn't a lot of light.

But she said, "Want to come inside?"

"Inside?" I repeated it stupidly. I hadn't taken shelter inside a building since the night I left Bishop's Close.

She nodded at the door. "This is my place."

My thoughts flew. She might take me in only to hit me on the head in order to rob me. There might be others in there, violent people. God knew what they'd do to me.

I asked, "Who's in there?"

"Eh?"

"Who else is in there?"

"Nobody. Just me."

That seemed so unlikely I found it hard to believe her. I nearly ran.

What would my life have been if I had run from Darcy that night? I'd likely have ended in the workhouse after all or died of starvation on the streets, only to be buried in this same place where I now lie. Maybe the end was forecast after all.

She decided for me, just as she would so often in the future. "Come on."

She shouldered past me and opened the door onto thick, deep darkness. The place smelt musty and felt cold, but no one else was there. I followed her in.

No question but stepping over that threshold meant stepping into a new life. With those few, faltering paces everything changed.

Darcy moved ahead of me and struck a light. I smelled the sulfur cutting through the damp fugue.

"Come on then," she said impatiently. "Shut the door."

Once she'd lit the stub of a candle, I saw the place must be deserted, and I could tell why. The door might be stout enough, but part of the roof had fallen in along with a center wall, now just a rubble of bricks. The state of the building accounted for the damp and the smell, but even if it lay open for the most part to the sooty sky at least we were out of sight, enclosed in brick arms.

"What happened here?" I wondered aloud.

"Fire in the chimney and the whole stack gave way, came down on the roof. A woman died here, so I heard."

"Oh." I looked at her, able to see her now in the yellow candle flame. Impossible to tell how old Darcy might be. She said later she was sixteen, but she didn't look it, and she lied about a lot of other things. I never knew what to believe. I said, "A woman died in the last place I lived also."

She shrugged. Shorter than me and wizened, she had brown hair and, in daylight, blue eyes. Her face might have been that of any girl in the East End—pale, snub-nosed, and entrenched with a certain belligerence. Her cheeks and forehead were marked by a few sores— in that light I took them for the blemishes that mark us all. Not a pretty face, but I saw there a certain hard radiance.

"Nobody comes here or bothers you?" I asked.

"Only those wot I let in. Look at this." She pulled from one pocket a curious object, narrow and stubby.

"What's that?"

"My knife. I made it, and I'll stick anybody who pesters me."

That filled me with admiration, and I instantly wanted a knife like it for the reassurance it might lend.

"So." She had been eyeing me even as I examined her. "Wot's a piece like you doin' out on the street?"

"A piece like me?" I repeated. Was I different from anyone else?

She sniffed. "You got a look about you, like you been taken care of."

Astute was Darcy to see through the dirt, hunger, and despair.

"Wot's yer name?" she asked.

"Polly Bridger."

"I'm Darcy Wilkins. You can stay here the night if you like, so long as you tell me your story."

I shot another doubtful look around the room, if such it could be called. It constituted shelter of a sort. Rats might well live here.

I might, but only if she let me.

That balance—that inference—was clear from the start. But God help me, so desperate was I that I stayed.

Chapter Thirteen

"So, Polly Bridger, are you hungry?" Darcy inquired.

Better to ask if it rained in London, if the fog came in from the river to choke a girl while she slept, if men relieved themselves in alleyways.

I nodded.

She went over to the pile of rubble and climbed up. A sack hung there, only dimly seen. She took it down and told me, "Go on, sit. I'll give you something."

I could not guess what might lie in the sack—it might be moldy cheese or a severed head. But I began to salivate.

There was cheese, hard but not moldy, and a bit of bread. She offered some to me.

"Eat slow," she advised, "or your belly will hurt something fierce. How long since you ate?"

I shook my head, mouth too full of cheese to answer. She spoke truly—the apples I stole frequently gave me fierce stomach pains. Hunger kept me from caring.

She watched me in silence for several moments while I ate before she pushed, "How did you end up sleeping on my doorstep?"

Her doorstep. Oh, what luxury to have a place, even one like this, to call your own.

"My parents and little sister all died one after

t'other. My husband was looking after me—"

"'Usband!" she interrupted. "You married?"

"Yes." I told her gravely, "As good as."

She nodded soberly. "He died too?"

"No, in prison."

"Ah." She made it into a sound of commiseration. "How long?"

"He got three years."

Her sharp gaze slid over me. "You pregnant?"

"No." Albert and I had never…well, done what it took to start a babe.

"Good. It rarely ends well, does that."

"I've been looking for work," I told her earnestly. "No one will take me on. And I've thought about the workhouse."

"You don't want to go there."

"At least they feed you, don't they? There's a roof and walls."

"None you'd want around you. You'd be better off in prison, almost."

Hesitantly I asked, "You been inside the workhouse?"

"Only when I was small. My ma died there."

"Oh. I'm sorry."

"She went there and took me with her, only 'cause she was sick. They worked her anyway, and hard. And they separated us. I wasn't even with her when she died."

"After—after that you didn't stay?"

"Ran away, didn't I? Just like you'd escape Hell."

I believed her. Hard to imagine it could be worse inside the workhouse than on the cold streets, but yes, I did believe her.

"So," I asked, "what's to do?"

She shrugged. "There's Ma Clark."

"Who's that, then?"

"You ain't heard of Ma Clark? Cor, you have been sheltered. She takes girls like you in."

"A charity, like?" I brightened. Might this be the answer?

"Not a charity. She takes you in and you work for her."

"Doing what?"

"Don't you know nothin'? You're like a babe, you are."

I gazed at her solemnly.

"You gotta work," Darcy said. "We all work to live. It's how you go about it that matters."

I nodded as if I understood. I didn't.

Darcy sighed. "Ma Clark puts you on the streets. Earning." An aged, wise look came to Darcy's face. "But then she takes a part of the earnings, a big part. Room and board she calls it. I was with her a while. But I decided I could do better on me own."

"But—earning how?"

"Don't you know nothing? I thought you said you was married."

Oh. She was talking about what Ma had traded to Mr. Grimp in order to keep our room. Horror drenched me, clammy and cold. No, not that.

"I'd rather be in the workhouse."

"That's what you think. Want to pull apart oakum with torn and bloody fingers?"

"What's oakum?"

"It's this stiff rope that slices your skin to shreds. When last I saw Ma—across the yard it was—she'd no skin at all left on her fingers."

"Still, it's got to be better than letting men, strange men—"

"Poke you? I dunno. Maybe it is and maybe it isn't. Over pretty quick, usually. But then there's the pox."

"You mean small pox?"

"No, the French pox." Darcy touched her face. "See? It's not real bad yet. I know girls who've lost most their noses and look a real fright."

I thought of Betty at the match factory, her teeth showing through her cheek. I shuddered.

"Why would you—"

"'Cause it's on my terms, see? I choose who and when. I got a string of regulars, so they ain't strangers, are they?"

"Is that how you catch this French pox?"

"Yeah, but everybody gets it. Just a matter of time."

"Does it go away?"

Darcy gave me a sharp smile. "Some folk say there's a cure. The surest cure's the grave."

"It can kill you?"

"Don't everything?"

****

I stayed with Darcy that night and the next, and the one after that, and she never demanded anything of me. At the time I didn't ask why. I was too happy being off the streets, even if I was a rat in a hole.

I've wondered since, of course, why she took me in, whether it was out of pity as I first supposed. I think I know better now, but I hate to believe it. Darcy was my one friend, and it's difficult to accept she would betray me.

Yet it wasn't betrayal, was it? Darcy showed me a means to survive while Albert was shut away. She didn't make me accept that path.

I had the best sleep I'd enjoyed since I left Bishop's Close that night, and I dreamed of Albert.

I dreamed he came home to me, walked down the alley into the Close as I'd longed for him to do so many times, straight and tall, his hair gleaming ginger in the sun. My relief at seeing him felt very real. Like a girl reborn I ran to meet him, and we embraced right out in the open. But no one saw, for we were the only ones there.

"Is your time up?" I squealed. "Is it up?"

"No. No, Pol."

"Then how is it you're here?"

"The walls of the prison dissolved. I walked out."

"So easy as that? How did they dissolve?"

"I wished on it."

I gasped. "If only you'd known sooner. You could have come to me weeks ago."

"I'm here now, Pol. Everything will come right." We gazed into one another's eyes, and I beheld his light—banked and simmering but there sure enough. His time inside hadn't destroyed it. Gratitude brought tears to my eyes.

"But what's this?" Gently, he touched my cheek. "Pol, what have you done to yourself?"

I woke abruptly and I can tell you, I knew the disappointment of that being just a dream. For I'd felt his arms around me and his finger on my cheek.

But I still lay in the rubble of Darcy's place. We slept beneath the part of the ceiling that hadn't collapsed, a corner with brick walls standing three stories high like broken teeth, stretching above. Cold daylight and fog all came drifting in.

I sat up, my head swimming. Darcy still slept not an arm's reach away from me, and I took the opportunity to look at her.

The sores on her face—I learned later they were properly called lesions—centered mostly around her nose and on her forehead. One reached up into her hair. I wondered how bad they hurt and how fast they spread.

I wondered what Albert saw on my face in the dream.

Asleep, Darcy lost her hardness, her edge. She looked young and almost pretty. Just a girl after all.

I sat quietly till she woke. Then she went out and got us some breakfast. Those first three days she provided for me without comment. She went out each day around four of the clock, when it started to get dark and came back some time in the earliest hours of the morning after she'd done—well, whatever she had to do.

Daytimes, we talked. I hadn't had anyone to whom I could talk properly in a long while. Albert and I used to talk like that up in my room, lying hand in hand. Now after Darcy woke up—for she slept late into the day—we told one another about our pasts, which had faded away.

I felt as happy to listen as to speak. Inexpressibly grateful to her, I accepted that once she'd been like me, a girl child with parents who loved her. A good girl despite everything.

I confided in her about Albert's and my relationship, but I'm not sure she believed me. She possessed but one currency for survival, and I don't think she fathomed that Albert would look after me without me paying it to him.

"He loved me," I tried to explain. "He loves me yet."

She'd eyed me in consideration. "I can understand that. You're awfully pretty, ain't you?"

Was I still? I didn't feel it.

"But a man's a man, right? They all wants one thing."

Albert had wanted to keep me safe. I knew that, to my bones.

She thought about what I'd said and at last told me, "Why, Pol, you've got a valuable commodity there."

"What's that?"

"Something so rare on these streets, it's barely heard of. There are gentlemen will pay a lot of money for a girl who's not been touched."

Gentlemen? I couldn't imagine any man who did to Darcy what her regulars did being called by such a name. But I asked, "Why?"

"'Cause they believe it's one of the cures, see?"

"Cures?"

"For the pox. They think giving a poke to a girl who's all clean and fresh can take it away."

"Can it?"

"Don't think so. I know plenty blokes who've tried it and seem no better. But they believes it, don't they? So they'll pay through the nose—if they still got one." She gave a hard laugh. "Girl as pretty as you could ask a high price, all right."

"But—I don't want to do that."

"Ain't nobody wants to. But I can't feed you forever. And how d'you think I'm earning your bread?"

I considered leaving then so I would not be a burden on her. But I could not make myself face the specter of the streets, did not want to give up the dubious safety of even these rickety walls.

As I've learned, even an illusion of safety is better than none at all.

Chapter Fourteen

"I knows a bloke," Darcy said one afternoon. "A right gentleman."

I looked at her uncertainly. We shared a late breakfast—more like dinner really—and I felt grateful enough to listen to whatever she wished to say. But I'd already learned the word *gentleman*, for her, equaled one of her regulars as she also called them.

She seemed to have developed relationships with these men, to feel somewhat comfortable with them. I couldn't imagine how.

"His name's Mr. Spencer. At least that's what he tells me. I doubt many of them go by their real names when they're in our part of town."

I said nothing, just crammed a bit of bread into my maw.

"I been speaking to him about you," Darcy went on casually.

"You have?"

"Yes indeed."

"Why?"

"He's well-padded, ain't he?"

"Eh?"

"He's got some brass. He could pay well." She considered it. "He *would* pay well."

"For what?" I shouldn't have asked. I knew. I wasn't so green as all that. My stomach turned, and the bread stuck in my throat. "Does he have it—the pox?"

She gazed at me a long time as if she thought about lying. Darcy lied a lot, though I didn't know it then.

At last she said, "Yes. Most o' them do. That's why he'd pay so much, see? He's quite far along and desperate for a cure."

"He thinks I'd be a cure?"

"He hopes so. I told him how clean you are. And you're pretty as well. You could make a killing."

A killing. But…killing whom?

"How much?" I asked against my better judgment.

"I reckon enough to keep us for months."

Us. The implication spoke loudly: she'd been keeping me. I needed to return the favor.

"I don't think I could."

"We can do lots of things we thought we couldn't. And he's safe, like. Won't beat you or knife you, and he always pays."

"Would I catch it? From him."

Again she hesitated as if she considered a falsehood before she shrugged. "Probably. Maybe not, if it's just the once."

"Does it hurt?"

"Eh?"

"Those sores." I gestured at her face. "The pox."

"The pain's not so bad. My pa used to whip us, before Ma took me and ran away from him—that's how we wound up in the poorhouse. Now, that hurt. But they say this gets worse as it moves along. The sores bite deep. That's why Mr. Spencer's so desperate to get better, right?"

"I still don't think I could."

She didn't press it then. She went out a little earlier

than usual that afternoon, and I crept out soon after. The streets were foggy and cold, but the fog hid me while I stole a few apples which I brought back to Darcy's to serve as my contribution.

Darcy slept long and woke late. When she rose, she fished some things out of her bag—a penny and a small glass bottle.

"What's that?" I asked.

"Mr. Spencer gave it me in lieu of pay. Right expensive, this is."

"What is it, though?"

"Mercury. For the pox, see? It can be treated. So"—she fixed me with her shrewd blue eyes—"you've no need to be afeared."

But I was afeared. I watched as she opened the tiny bottle and spilled a few drops of silvery liquid into a cup of ale. This she drank.

"I need to sleep some more," she said then. "You take that penny and go buy us food."

I did as bidden, both then and later.

****

I wish I could say Darcy did not press me. She was my friend, my one friend, and my sole source of security. I suppose that knowledge provided pressure all on its own.

A week passed and then another. I lived off Darcy as a louse lives off a scalp. Oh, I cadged a few things out on the street but nothing of much value.

Meanwhile she swore to me the mercury medicine was working, even though she finished what was in the tiny bottle and got no more.

I waited for the sores on her face to fade. They didn't, but neither did they get any worse.

I tried to think of ways I might persuade her to look after me till Albert got out of jail, but it seemed a long time, so very long.

Then one night she brought him home with her, Mr. Spencer.

She'd never before done anything of the kind, and it shocked me to my toes. I was sleeping when they arrived, but I leaped up swiftly, staring in disbelief.

I suppose I'd built up a picture of this Mr. Spencer, gentleman, in my mind. The truth proved nothing like my imaginings.

Seen on the street he might indeed have been taken for an ordinary gentleman, except for the sores, of course. Much worse than Darcy's, they fair mottled his face, which must have been homely at best.

Not above middle height, he had a narrow countenance and thinning hair. He was well dressed to be associating with the likes of Darcy, and had an almost courtly manner. His nose should also have been long—bony—but part of it was gone, eaten away by those sores that clawed their way up across his forehead and into his scalp.

I will confess I stared in horror. I'd seen worse, I suppose, on the streets. But I'd never touched anyone so affected. I couldn't imagine Darcy doing so or wishing for me to.

For I was not quite the fool she supposed me. It was why they had come.

"All right, Polly?" Darcy said in a sweet, sickening voice I'd never heard her employ.

It was not all right. I'd felt safe here. Now I did not know what to think.

Darcy went on, "I've brought someone who would

like to meet you."

Mr. Spencer smiled at me. It might have been a pleasant enough smile at one time—no longer.

"Good evening, Miss Polly. Miss Darcy has told me all about you."

I shot Darcy an accusing look. *How could you?* But as if she played at something, at being someone else, she ignored it.

"Mr. Spencer has been ever so anxious to make your acquaintance."

I did not ask why. I knew why. He wanted from me what he'd got from Darcy, what Ma had traded to Mr. Grimp.

I backed up a few steps, clutching my blanket tight around me.

They began a conversation between the two of them.

"You can see what I said, Mr. S. She ain't been out on the streets. At least not doin' anything she shouldn't."

"I see," Mr. Spencer agreed.

"Barely knows the score. Untouched."

"Exquisite. Miss Darcy, I am certainly most interested."

They discussed me as if I were a piece of meat. As if I hung in the market.

"A cure, unquestionably," Mr. Spencer murmured. "What will it take?"

"Dunno." Darcy shot me a judicious look. "Some considerable persuasion."

Mr. Spencer took a step forward. "Miss Polly, I wish very much for us to be friends, as I am with Miss Darcy now. She can tell you how beneficial I may be to my friends. I can provide things. Money, clothing. Medicine."

My mind screamed warnings at me. I would not need medicine if I kept away from him.

But I did need money. Everyone needed money.

"'Tis a hard world out there," he went on softly, almost soothingly. "A young girl needs a protector. I could be that for you."

I wanted to say I already had a protector—my Albert, who was my everything. But the words stuck in my throat.

"Mr. Spencer's right generous," Darcy put in. "And you can see he's not frightenin', like some of the gents."

How could she look into this man's ruined face and say that? The very sight of him terrified me.

"I treat my young ladies very well and would much like to further an acquaintance with you, Miss Polly."

I wanted to run. I should have run then. What might have happened if I had? Would I still have ended up here, where I now lie? Maybe not, or maybe so. From what Darcy said, it was inevitable.

Three years is such a long time.

Mr. Spencer fished in his pocket and came up with a coin. It glinted bright in the shadowy room. This he held out to me. "Here, my dear. Take this as a show of my regard."

I did not want to touch that coin, which he'd had about his person. Besides, accepting it might put me under obligation to him.

I shook my head.

"Don't be a fool, girl." Darcy it was who snatched the coin and pressed it into my balled fist.

"An investment," Mr. Spencer told me, "in our future friendship."

I saw him slip Darcy a similar coin. Ah, they conspired together! Before I could catch her eye they turned toward the door. He was leaving. Relief made me light in the head.

"I am not disappointed," I heard him say to Darcy before he went out. "I will see you tomorrow night, my dear."

She ushered him out like a lady escorting a visitor from her good sitting room. I realized he'd paid to meet me.

Just to meet me.

When Darcy turned back, the simpering look slid from her face. I expected her to scold me, to bully me and try to force me into doing what Mr. Spencer wanted.

Instead, despair filled her eyes. "Polly, I know this ain't what you want."

"How could you bring him here? How?" I'd felt so safe.

She shrugged uncomfortably. "My place, innit? I've earned it. And d'you know how?" She jerked her head at the door. "He's how. And others like him. He's the best of the lot, and I'm willing to share him with you."

"His face—"

She made an odd movement, a full body shudder. "You gets used to it." She touched her own cheek. "You has to."

"He paid you to bring him here," I accused, "You betrayed me."

"I'm trying to help you, silly girl. Look at the

coin."

I didn't want to. It felt ugly in my hand. It felt as diseased at Mr. Spencer.

"Look at it. You ever seen one of those?"

A gold sovereign. My head swam again. It couldn't be.

Darcy stepped closer. "Listen to me. Your husband's not coming back right quick, and you're goin' to have to keep yourself. That's the truth. You need to face it. Mr. Spencer's not like what you'd find out on the streets. You go to Ma Clark, she'll take what you earn. On your own, men will beat you and sometimes they won't pay. Terrible things can happen. Girls get cut up, they die. You should thank me for introducing you to him."

"I don't want to get what he's got." *What you've got*, but I didn't add that.

"Come early or late," she almost sang the words, "it comes to us all."

Chapter Fifteen

I ached for Albert then. I wished with all my heart I might speak with him for just five minutes and ask him what to do, and how to survive in his absence. I would have gone to the place where he was if I could, would have walked there if only to see the steady light in his gray eyes. That light, so I believed, had the power to save me.

But I was not sure of his direction, didn't know if he'd been kept at Newgate to serve his sentence or sent elsewhere.

So the next day I gave Darcy my gold piece. It might have been a foolish thing to do, and I thought about it a long time while she slept into the late afternoon.

I might have run off and lived on that coin for a spell. But time, as I'd discovered, was an inexorable force and always moved on. When I came to the end of the money, what then? It would not last three years.

So I gave it to a sleepy Darcy and said, "To pay my way here. So I won't have to—"

That opened her eyes right enough. She didn't argue it, just tucked the coin away in her clothing, leaving me with nothing—except, so I hoped, a measure of security.

I had no concept of the value of a gold piece and no idea how long a time it might buy me under Darcy's roof. But two weeks passed before she so much as mentioned Mr. Spencer again.

I do know what she bought with what he'd given her. She brought home two vials of the medicine and laid it out on the floor.

"That's the cure?" I asked, peering over her shoulder. "What did you say it's called?"

"Mercury. See how pretty it is?" She leaned aside so I could watch the substance drop into a cup. Silvery it was, and thick. "Anything that pretty's bound to make a girl pretty again, innit?"

I shot her a look. Darcy never mentioned her appearance and acted most times as if it didn't matter to her. But it must.

The mercury might be pretty, but did that mean it would put rout to the ugly sores? I hoped so. Darcy had been kind to me. And she represented my only refuge.

I wondered if Mr. Spencer took mercury. He certainly must have money enough, if he handed out gold sovereigns so readily. Why hadn't it cured his disease?

I did not ask, for I thought I saw hope in Darcy's eyes, and as I'd learned, sometimes hope is all a girl has.

****

That winter proved a hard one, rough and merciless. No one bothered us there in our little bolt hole, though once a crew of workers came down the alley and entered the building through a door farther along.

Darcy, who was home at the time, it being early afternoon, whispered that they meant to take the building down eventually, and I could feel my security once more begin slipping away from me. But after their inspection the crew went away, and I saw them not again.

Snow found us through the open roof of our lair if it turned cold enough, or rain the rest of the time. The rain, filthy with coal grit, soiled everything it touched. We seldom felt warm. Darcy took a wicked cough that roused her even when she slept.

She also continued to dose herself with the mercury, at least until it ran out. I did not notice much improvement to the lesions on her skin. Neither did they worsen, so I supposed the cure worked slowly and she held her own against the sickness.

I never asked what she did with the coin I gave her. I supposed she spent it on food or coal. She always brought home something for us to eat and shared most fairly with me. And once or twice she brought fairy cakes she said Mr. Spencer had sent.

Thus I knew she still saw him. But weeks went by before she once more pressed me to befriend him, as she put it.

Once, when she felt too ill with the ague to go out and work, we got to talking. I remember she lay in her bundle of blankets and I sat beside her, both of us huddled under the remaining portion of the ceiling. I watched snowflakes come swirling down to land like white feathers in the room. I wondered where Albert was just then and if he thought of me.

Darcy moved restlessly and said, "I think I have fever."

"Sleep for a while," I bade her. We'd been talking about the people we'd known in our lives, which was what had brought Albert so strongly to mind. In truth, he always dwelt in my thoughts, having a home there, but this brought him to the forefront.

"I can't sleep," she complained and coughed again.

"Would you like a dose of your medicine?" I knew by now how to measure it out. I'd get her a hot drink but just then we had no coal for a fire. Still, I assured myself, it was better than the streets.

"It's nearly gone." She stared bleakly into the near distance.

I dared to ask, "Do you think it's helping?"

"I don't know, Pol, truly I don't. My sores are no worse."

I knew—for I'd seen—she had them on her face and also on her scalp beneath her hair, and on her legs too.

"Do they hurt a lot?"

She must have been in a rare mood indeed, for she gave me the truth. "They bother me a good bit, Pol, but not like you'd think from the look of 'em. Yet they take a terrible hold on a lass and burn right down into the bone. A horrid way to end, innit? An awful end, indeed."

Fear blossomed in my heart. I couldn't lose her, I simply couldn't. She was all I had, with Albert away.

"You aren't anywhere near your end," I told her staunchly. "You're just feeling low from the cough."

Ignoring my words, she went on, "Sometimes I can't sleep from thinking about it. How the dark will come down and I won't know nothing more. That's what happens, you know. It will drive me fair mad. Folk do go mad from this. They say the sores turn your brain and send you raving even if the worry don't."

"Won't the mercury stop it before then?"

"Maybe. Maybe no."

"Let me mix you some. Tomorrow, stay in again and rest. I'll go out to get something for your cough."

"We daren't spend much, if I'm not earning."

"I can pick something up." *Picking up* was my term for stealing, and I'd become fairly good at it. I stole to supplement our diet mostly.

She nodded.

"Try and sleep," I urged again, and she quieted. But even when she fell asleep her limbs jerked, and she moaned from the evil dreams.

****

Those who lie around me here in my poor grave grow ever more silent. It is as if the life trickles slowly from them bit by bit, and the peace deepens. I can feel the life draining from me also. I wonder if soon I will no longer remember my story or be able to think about it.

Polly Bridger. I am Polly Bridger, only nineteen years old.

I can barely feel the bared chest of my neighbor beneath my shoulder, or the limbs flung over mine. But from time to time an interruption occurs. There comes the scrape, scrape, scrape of iron tools on stony dirt, our shared grave is opened, and another body is laid in with us to share this space, this new home.

Then for a brief time, the light floods in upon me. Being the light of London, it looks tarnished with coal smoke, but it is beautiful all the same. How I love the light! I wish I could rise into it free of all pain and just fly.

Soon the gritty soil comes down upon us once more, and we subside into the quiet. I can feel emotions from the new arrival—restlessness or bewilderment, sometimes grief.

Often, though—so often—there is relief. Here we stop struggling, we stop fighting.

And there's no pain. Darcy didn't speak the whole truth to me that day. The legacy of the pox includes pain both of the body and the mind. Gone, now.

But the price seems equally hard to bear, for surrendering the pain meant surrendering my life.

If only I might have been with Albert just one more time.

Chapter Sixteen

Darcy's ague passed at last, and her health in general seemed to improve. I thought for sure the mercury cure must be working, for she had more energy, and the light that lurked at the back of her eyes once more strengthened.

The weather also improved, the cold loosening its icy grip and the snow changing to persistent rain.

I continued to go out thieving, though I also still looked for work—a legitimate job, that is. But I'd become even more raggedy by now, and no respectable employer would agree to hire me.

When I returned to the match factory, I was once more told to clear off, and there was no penny this time.

It must have been March when Darcy came home early one morning and said, "Mr. Spencer's been asking after you."

"Has he?" Dread settled in my stomach like a lump of hot lead.

"Oh, yes. You might think he's forgotten you. He ain't forgotten."

Forgetting, as I knew, was hard. The memories crept right into your dreams. Sometimes I dreamed I lay in bed with Albert again, our fingers linked. Sometimes I dreamed I scrubbed Ma's blood from the floor back in our room at Bishop's Close.

If you'd asked me then what I might want for my

life—had I dared want anything—I would have replied first to see Albert, to be with him. And second, to forget.

"Mr. Spencer, he asks if you've changed your mind. He bade me tell you he'll pay handsomely." She looked at me, bleak light in her eyes. "For just the one time. You'd only have to do it once."

For an instant I felt trapped, hopeless, the brick walls of the ruined building we shared toppling in on me. Was this thing inevitable? Had I no choice?

"You see," Darcy went on, "he truly believes you're the cure. His cure."

"But what if I'm not? And what if I catch it from him instead of curing him? You keep saying I wouldn't catch it just the once, but what if I do? What would Albert say when he gets out?"

She shrugged. "He won't be out for—what, two and a half year? What you going to do till then?"

Swiftly I changed the subject. "Did you get more medicine?" She'd been all out and had fretted over it.

She nodded. "Mr. Spencer gave me some."

It occurred to me then to wonder, had he given her the medicine in exchange for her trying once more to persuade me? But Darcy remained my friend.

"Does it hurt, doing what Mr. Spencer wants?" I asked, just as I had about her disease. I remembered Ma's face, white with endurance when Mr. Grimp came to see her.

"Getting poked, you mean?"

I nodded.

She hesitated before she said, "Maybe a bit at first. After that, not so much. And it's over quick. You gets used to it."

You got used to a lot of things, so I'd learned. Being cold, being hungry. But you never got used to missing those you love.

I wondered then if I should consider Mr. Spencer's offer. I wondered if there were any other choices for me.

****

Time continued its inevitable march. Darcy kept going out to work. Still again, she ran out of medicine.

A funny thing about Darcy. I'd never met anyone so strong, other than Albert. And like him she carried the light, though hers was trapped and hard as a shard of glass, whereas his had flowed out to embrace me. Mostly she treated me kindly and with patience. I never did succeed in figuring out why she'd admitted me to her life when she shut everyone else away, save for her gentlemen.

Sometimes she became irritable or downright irascible, though never with me directly. I did not take it personal.

I always supposed her illness affected her during these times, for she would moan in her sleep the most then, and rub fitfully at her legs. I wondered a time or two, when she threw things around the room, if the madness had begun to set in. What would I do if she turned mad?

I once suggested she see a physician, and she returned, "A quack, you mean?"

"No, a physician. Maybe Mr. Spencer could give you the money."

She laughed. "Not many physicians willing to see the likes of us, are there?"

"I don't know. There must be some who treat the

poor."

"The poor, my dear, are left alone to die. Young and old alike. No one wants to treat us. Nobody wants to know."

Late in April she once more brought up the subject of me seeing Mr. Spencer. She had a string of gentlemen, I knew, but rarely mentioned any of the others by name.

"Mr. Spencer, he's back asking after you. Desperate he is, to end his suffering."

"Is he getting worse? Does he not take the mercury?"

She gave me one of her looks. "Here's the thing with the mercury. Sometimes it works, sometimes it don't."

"You keep taking it."

"I'm not getting any worse, am I?"

I didn't feel so sure. I thought how she cried out during the night.

"Thing is," she said, "he's willing to pay big for your company, enough to keep us, like, even if we have to move out of here."

"Will we have to move?" I didn't want to, feeling comfortable with the place. As I've learned, it didn't take much to make a location feel like a home. And it was pleasant enough now, without the snow blowing in.

She nodded. "Word is they'll start knocking these old houses down now the weather is better."

"Where will we go?"

She shrugged. "Mr. Spencer says if you be friendly with him, he'll give us rent."

Rent. It always came down to the rent. I thought again of what Ma had done in exchange for it. I seemed to hear her voice in my mind.

Sometimes, Polly, we have to do what we don't want to do.

I shuddered. Then I asked Darcy, "Where would this thing—between me and Mr. Spencer—take place? Here?"

"Lord, no. In his carriage, most like. Or a hansom, driving around."

I tried to imagine it, being shut into the dark interior of a moving carriage with Mr. Spencer. But I didn't truly want to imagine it.

"Come on, Pol," Darcy said softly. "First time's the worst."

And I replied, "I'll think on it, right? Tell him that."

Even now, lying here in this quiet, I wonder what I could have done differently. I'd tried to find work. I'd have gone to the match factory to keep myself respectable. Albert seemed so far from me both in distance and time. I had no one else—no one save Darcy.

I ask you fairly, what could I have done different?

****

So it occurred, this act that in the end proved my death sentence. I am not proud of it, except maybe a little proud of my fortitude. For it wasn't easy. I was frightened near witless, and yet I made myself go through with the deed.

Darcy and Mr. Spencer arranged it all between them—the day, or rather the night—and the price. She took me to the assigned corner, and we stood waiting. I remember how my legs shook beneath me so I thought I would fall down before the carriage rolled into sight.

I tried to think of Albert then, but my mind shied away from him. He would not want this. I did not want it. But it was survival.

A hansom cab drew up, all black and shiny from the rain earlier. I have never since been able to look at a hansom without my stomach cramping. Death on wheels, they look to me.

The door opened, and Mr. Spencer looked out.

In a panic, I turned to Darcy. "I can't."

"Thousands do."

"Come on, girl," Mr. Spencer called.

I did not want to climb up into that cab. Every instinct bade me flee. But once again I heard my mother's voice speak in my head.

Polly, sometimes we all have to do what we don't want to do.

"Go on." Darcy gave me a little push. "I'll see you after."

I will not describe what happened inside that cab— I will not, except to say I did climb up and in. Mr. Spencer gave me a pouch of coins, which I tucked most carefully into the pocket of my coat—the same coat Albert had given me that always felt like his arms wrapped around me. Mr. Spencer said something—I don't remember what—and the cab began moving around the streets. I did as Mr. Spencer instructed me.

Darcy was wrong, though. She'd promised it would be quick. It wasn't. In a terrible way, it seemed to go on forever. And throughout, I had but one thought in my mind.

Make it stop, make it stop, make it stop, make it stop, make it—

Then, at last, it did stop. Mr. Spencer adjusted his

clothing and said, "Thank you, my dear. Will you agree to see me again?"

"No," I gasped and shook my head violently. "Darcy said—she said once."

"All right." He sounded so calm, given what had just taken place between us. "I will set you down at your corner."

No other words were exchanged. We drove for a while before the cab stopped. I could not get out of it fast enough.

I could see Darcy nowhere. I stood there while the cab drove off, my fingers closed around the precious pouch of coins in my pocket for which I'd just traded everything.

Darcy stepped from the shadows. "All right, duck?"

I began to cry.

"Here now, don't take on. You got paid?"

I nodded.

"That's all right, then."

But it wasn't. Nothing would ever be all right again.

Chapter Seventeen

Darcy found a room in a tenement some streets away from where we'd spent the winter. It must have been May when we moved there, or maybe early June. She paid the rent out of my earnings, and we lived on the rest.

You must understand I did not hand it all over to her as I had the gold coin. I'd earned that money in the most unspeakable way and intended to keep hold of it. But she'd been supporting me since winter, and when she asked for the rent, well—it's always about the rent, isn't it?

I liked the new room well enough, but the neighbors were noisy. I could hear the family to one side arguing nights while Darcy was out working. It sounded like the husband meant to kill the wife, a small, mousy woman of whom I'd caught glimpses. And sometimes I could hear through the wall the sound of him doing to her what Mr. Spencer had done to me.

I feared I'd end up like Ma, only with Mr. Spencer's brat in my belly. When it became evident that had not happened—thank God—I fretted I'd taken the pox.

"How can you tell if you've got it?" I asked Darcy repeatedly. "How long does it take?"

"You won't get it, the once." She gave me a speculative look. "Or even a couple times. It took me forever to get sick."

"So," I fretted, "how will I know?"

"You might get a little sore someplace, but it will go away soon enough."

With these careless words she shrugged the matter off, and eventually I calmed a bit. But we hadn't been in our new digs a month before she came home one morning and said, "Pol, there's another gentleman."

"What?" I stared at her. Heaven help me, for a minute I didn't know what she meant. The expression in her eyes told me. "No," I said.

"Pol—"

"You promised it would be once, just the once."

"Yeah. But look at the money you made."

"I don't care." I wrapped my arms tight around myself.

"That was a lot of dosh. Just for such a simple thing."

"Not so simple." Not at all. *Make it stop, make it stop.*

"This Mr. Guernsey, see, he's a young gent, younger than Mr. Spencer. He wants the cure."

"What?" I repeated. "But you said it only works if—if a girl's never been touched."

"Yeah, but Mr. Guernsey won't know you've already been round the block, will he? You still look good. Not a mark on you."

"That's lying. Plus he won't get healed." A thought occurred to me. "Is Mr. Spencer better?"

"Too soon to tell. Speaking of Mr. Spencer, he still wants to see you again. I was thinking, Pol, if you took on just one or two gentlemen regular—"

That made me wonder, did she just want to use me

the way Ma Clark used her girls? But that thought felt disloyal. Darcy was my one friend. She cared about me.

"I don't like to."

She snorted. "It's not about what we like, is it? It's about food in our bellies and paying the rent."

"Please, Darcy, no."

"You think about it," she said sternly for her. "Mr. Guernsey will pay near as good as old Spencer did. I been bargaining hard over you. So you just think about it."

****

I walked back to Bishop's Close while I was thinking and peered into the yard. I don't know what I was hoping to see there—a glimmer of light maybe. Someone who knew Albert or had word of him.

The place looked and smelled the same. Children wailed and ran about, women argued, and the toilets stank. At first I saw nobody I knew. Then I caught sight of Danny Pete amid a crowd of other boys.

It took a lot for me to walk down the alley into that yard. Folk stared, but when Danny saw me, he jogged over.

"Wot you doing here, Polly Bridger?"

He'd grown a little and was now taller than me. Rail thin, too, and dressed in rags, his face dirty. He seemed to sum me up as quickly—the now-tattered blue coat, my tangled hair.

I cleared my throat and said, "I've come to ask if you have any word of Albert."

His eyes clouded. I thought I saw grief there that near matched my own.

"Old Al's gone away for three years. I thought you knew that."

"I did, but where? Which prison? Have you got to see him?"

"He's been kept back in Newgate," Danny answered. "I wouldn't go near that place on a bet."

But he looked after you, I thought in protest. He cared for all you lot. Don't you care in return?

I said, "I thought I'd try and go see him."

Danny's dour expression lightened a bit. "He'd like that, I reckon. But, Miss Polly, it's no place for the likes o' you."

The likes of me? Did he realize I'd lived on the streets? Did he know how low I'd sunk?

"How—how do I get in?"

His sharp gaze flickered over me again. "Best to go with money. Take a cab, if you can afford it."

A cab. I shuddered.

"Then you can bribe the guards. And leave a bit by to give Al—if you see him—that he can use it for bribes later."

"You mean if I have no dosh I can't see him?"

He shrugged.

Money. My heart thudded in my chest.

I looked away from Danny, afraid he might see the horror in my eyes and glanced at the buildings. "Is Mr. Grimp still landlord here?"

"O' course. You ain't been gone all that long."

"I need to get away." Before Grimp saw me.

"He ain't here now." Danny gave me a long stare before he dug in his pocket and presented tuppence. "You see Al, you give him that. From me."

Foolish tears rose to my eyes. So Danny did care. Such a small kindness to prompt such a response from me. But then, kindness had become a rare commodity.

"I will," I told Danny. "I certainly will."

****

I might claim I agreed to see Mr. Guernsey for Albert's sake, but that would be a lie and I would not so sully Albert's memory as to suggest it. In truth I agreed to see him not for the sake of the money alone but out of a queer sense of loyalty to Darcy. The fact that I wanted to spend the money in an effort to see Albert only served to make it bearable to me.

Only it proved unbearable after all, even though Darcy prepared me well for that encounter. She stole a dress for me to wear and worked for hours over my hair, using an old comb we shared.

I was to go to a meeting place, a room Mr. Guernsey procured, which terrified me. Darcy assured me she had arranged it all and would take me there and wait outside.

"How long?" I whispered on the night. "How long will I need to stay there?"

"Not long. Just like before, and I'll be right outside."

"Do you promise?"

"Yes. But for Gawd's sake don't let on that you've been with anyone else. Right? He thinks you haven't, and that's why he's willing to pay so much. So when it happens, act like it hurts and all."

In truth, I did not need to act. I did not like Mr. Guernsey, not one bit. Not that I favored Mr. Spencer either. But Mr. Guernsey—though much younger—was also much rougher, and it took longer there in the gloomy chamber.

I do not want to talk—or think—any more about it. Even now, lying here amid this quiet air of peace, I want to push the memory away from me, wall it off in that part of my mind where the terrible things lie.

After, I wept, which did not seem to surprise Mr. Guernsey. Neither did it please him. "Shut up, you silly chit," he told me and ordered me out.

Darcy had waited.

"Did he pay?" she asked immediately, and I nodded, Mr. Guernsey having shoved the money into my hand.

No other words passed between us that night. The next day, Darcy sat me down.

"Look, duck," she said, not unkindly, "there's no need to carry on. We does what we has to in this life, right? He wasn't so bad, was he?"

Every time I thought of Mr. Guernsey, I experienced a full body shudder. "He was sick, real sick." I'd never seen anyone so riddled with the pox, not then.

"Sure, well, that's why he was willing to pay so much, right? For the cure."

"I'll get sick, for sure."

"Maybe not."

"I don't want to see him again."

"Come on, Pol. Nobody's forcing you."

A lie, that. Life itself forced me.

"And I want to keep some of the money," I told her, "so I can go see Albert."

"You keep all of it if you want to."

That wouldn't be fair. There was still the rent to be covered. There was always the rent.

Chapter Eighteen

Soon after that I went to Newgate. Since Mr. Spencer, I could barely tolerate the sight of a hansom cab—they looked like death to me, black and all shiny in the wet—yet I made myself crawl inside one for the ride there. I wore my new dress, and terror held me in its grip the whole time.

By now it had been six months since I'd seen Albert. I felt proud I'd survived but not of how I'd survived. And I argued long in my head over what I should tell him.

I shouldn't have worried. Despite bribing a guard with my hard-earned coin, I was not permitted to see Albert. I never found out, then or later, why.

I did leave him a message and a small gift of money, entrusting both to the guard, who promised to deliver them. He stared at me with impassive eyes when I said, "Please tell him Polly Bridger remembers and loves him." I couldn't tell if the man meant to keep the promise.

I will admit I sank very low in spirit after that. Life, particularly since Ma's death, had not been easy, and all hope fled from me now. I could not seem to think straight, could scarcely think at all, and I went off my feed. Though Darcy brought home delicacies—even a savory pasty—I could not touch them. I slept away most of my time, seeking the oblivion that would not quite come. For sometimes I dreamed of Mr. Guernsey, and the horror of it would bring me awake, sweating.

Even from the depths of my misery I could tell something ailed Darcy—something beyond the usual, that was. Though her sores hadn't worsened, and she continued dosing herself with the mercury, a new ailment beset her, one that kept her from going out nights as she used to do.

It frightened me out of my own deep well of misery, a bit. If I lost Darcy, I did not know what I would do. She represented all security in my life, all warmth and wisdom.

I could see but one way to help her, to look after her the way she'd been looking after me. When she said Mr. Spencer had once more asked to see me, I agreed.

Again, I will not relay the details of what then became my life except to say Mr. Spencer was not the only one. I never would agree to see Mr. Guernsey, and for all I know he did not ask. For all I knew, he might be dead.

But I still showed no signs of disease, and Darcy was able to set high prices on my supposed virtue, bargaining it to other men as a possible cure.

All I had to do was pretend—and endure.

Did I feel shame? Oh, yes, you may be certain. I felt ashamed and dirty when I felt anything at all. For I am here to tell you, the senses become blunted. It is not so much that you stop minding—for I always did mind it—but that your capacity for feeling how much you mind it wears away.

For all that, I felt sick each and every time.

Mr. Spencer remained kind to me. Sometimes he gave me little presents, and he called me his Polly. I did

116

not tell him I would only ever belong to Albert Coward.

Do you suppose I forgot Albert then? Well I did not. He remained with me always, though there were times when my love for him retreated quite far into hiding.

There were also times I considered ending my life. There was always the river. The coppers were forever fishing bodies of girls like me out of the drink. But I thought if I meant to end the suffering, I would throw myself instead in front of a grand carriage and team.

I could not end my suffering, though, for what would happen when Albert finished serving his sentence and came looking for me? Because I knew to my very soul that he would.

I did not see Mr. Spencer—or any of the gentlemen—often. But even so, I could see that his disease progressed. Being with me had not cured him. He carried a miasmic odor, and I could scarcely bear to look into his ruined face.

Then come the fall, Darcy's symptoms abruptly worsened. Despite the fact that she spent our precious coin on mercury, her lesions spread and began to eat away at her face.

I'd also had a sore appear by then, down below. Just one little sore that went away swiftly enough. I showed no other symptoms. Not then.

I did however suffer other woes at the hands of Darcy's gentlemen. I caught some kind of fever, and it burned when I made water.

Unsympathetic—or perhaps merely caught in her own concerns—Darcy told me, "You need to put vinegar up there. That's the cure."

So I expended another precious coin for vinegar,

and a rough cure it proved to be.

A year came and went—a whole year since Albert had gone inside. Darcy and I tried to make a merry Christmas and failed dismally. The first of my lesions showed up then. I wept and wept, but there seemed no hope for it. After a year away from Bishop's Close, despair possessed me.

Darcy could no longer pass me off as unsullied—not given the fluid-filled sore that nestled beside my nose and those which climbed up my forehead. I might as well have worn a badge that read *Pox*. One that declared my death sentence.

Once I asked Darcy how she endured it, knowing how sick she was. We lay in our cots in the heat of the afternoon—for the room proved as hot in summer as it was cold in winter. I took a breath of the stifling air before I spoke.

"Darcy—how do you stand it? The staring faces when you go out and everyone knowing—knowing how you got it?"

She gave a laugh that held no humor. "You just wait till you look like me, Pol. What you've got—that's nothin', yet."

"I know." Still, people stared and, I fancied, condemned even though there were many, many others like me.

Darcy said, "I don't let myself think on it. I think more about other things, about the cure."

The cure wasn't working for her, though. Even I could see that. The disease seemed to progress steadily and inevitably once it began, and it gradually blotted out the light.

That winter Darcy told me Mr. Spencer was no

longer coming out—too ill, and starting to go mad. Madness, as she informed me, was one of the end stages of the pox. I felt sorry, even given what had passed between us. He'd always acted kindly toward me.

In February—a vile, wet month as it proved—Darcy brought home word she'd heard on the street. Mr. Spencer had died while tied to a bed and raving.

I wondered then if that would be my future also. Fear prompted me to take a bit of my hoarded cash and go to see a proper physician.

Darcy had learned of this physician at the local chapel. They had a graveyard there for the likes of such as we, not consecrated ground but adjacent to the proper graveyard and the church. It is, in fact, the same graveyard where I now lie. She heard there that Dr. Richards was one of the few who would agree to treat prostitutes.

I tried, in my mind, to deny that was what I'd become, a prostitute. For what would Pa have said? And Ma. What would Albert say if—when—he found out? But in the end I had to admit to it, at least I would when I went to see Dr. Richards and confessed how I'd caught the disease.

"Go," Darcy urged me. "Go now while we have the brass. Maybe it's still early enough for you."

We had become like sisters, caring for one another. I feared losing her almost as much as I feared Albert's absence. She might be hard-faced, yes, but I would never have survived without her. That's the simple truth.

So, eyes downcast, I went to see Mr. Richards, Physician. A young man with big hands and kindly eyes, he looked at me a long time and performed a ready examination.

"You have syphilis."

"Syph—I thought I had the French pox."

"It's the same. You've been on the streets?"

"Not much."

He grunted. "Enough."

My heart sank. I cannot tell you how it felt, sitting there in front of him, ashamed and frightened. "What was I to do?" I asked. "What else could I do?"

He shook his head.

"I'm going to die."

That made him lift his eyes once more to mine. Deep within his eyes, I caught a glimmer of light.

"How long?" I drew a breath. "How long do I have?"

"It's a slow disease. It can take years. But you see these lesions on your skin? They will go right down into the bone."

I did not need to see. I fancied I could feel them already, burrowing in. But…years. I would have time then to see Albert when he got out. If he wanted to see me, still.

I said, "My husband—"

Mr. Richards looked surprised. "You have a husband?"

"He's in Newgate. I want to live—live till he gets out."

"When will he get out?"

"A year and a half."

"You'll see him. But if you care about him, you won't have intercourse."

"Inter—?"

His stare made it plain what he meant.

"Oh," I babbled. "No. But tell me, Mr. Richards, is there no cure? No way I might be well before I see him? My friend, she takes mercury."

He clicked his tongue. "It is not a proper cure. And it's dangerous."

"Dangerous? How?"

"It creates an illness all its own." He named the symptoms—tremors, weakness, nausea, memory loss. Horrified, I realized Darcy had them all.

"Well, then, there must be some other cure for the pox."

"I'm sorry. There are all sorts of other things people try. I've seen no cures. Mercury, as I say, alleviates the symptoms but only for a time. It's a relentless disease."

"What can I do? I'll go mad, won't I? I don't want to go mad."

"Stay off the streets if you can. Try and keep the lesions clean. Pray."

Pray.

I'd lost my capacity for it. Prayer had not made Pa well or staunched the flow of Ma's blood. It could not halt this disease.

Kindly, Mr. Richards said, "Another word of advice—best not to get pregnant. It will not end well for you or the child."

I said the only thing I could. "Thank you. How much is your fee? I can pay—"

He waved off my offer of a coin. "Save it—buy yourself some good food. That may serve as well as the mercury."

"If I still want to try the mercury cure, should I buy

it from you?"

"I will not sell it to you, miss. I am all too certain it can be found on the black market. Just make sure you are purchasing the genuine article. You know what it looks like?"

"My friend takes it. Is there nothing else?"

"There's opium, but it's costly." He gave me a thin smile. "Most of my clients rely on gin."

Chapter Nineteen

Thereafter, I concentrated only on surviving the next year and a half. Nothing else meant much to me. I lived for the possibility of seeing Albert again.

Of course I knew not if he still lived or had perished there in Newgate. Fever, so we had heard, ran rampant there. If he lived, I told myself, he would find me.

And the time passed. Darcy's condition worsened mightily. She worked only rarely and saw but a few gentlemen. I also went out occasionally—in order to survive, you understand. I think part of me died each time. A measure of the light I'd stored up trickled away until I kept very little at all.

As Mr. Richards promised, my disease progressed slowly. When February of the following year arrived, I figured Albert had either been released or he was dead. I ached to know but hesitated to return to Bishop's Close and show my altered face.

Then in March, I ran an errand down the street and heard someone call my name.

"Polly Bridger! Miss Polly?"

I spun, mingled hope and dread rising in my heart, and saw Danny Pete standing on the opposite corner. He gestured wildly before, dodging carts and cabs, he dashed across.

There he got a good look at my face, and a sneer

touched his lips. Oh, so he thought the worse of me, did he? Had he ever tried to survive as a girl alone?

But his next words drove all thought from my mind. "Al's out. He's lookin' for you."

I could have fallen down where I stood. A great blossom of light exploded within me, followed by such dark shame I could scarcely endure it.

"Where? Where is he? At the Close?"

"No." Danny shook his head. "Not there. But he's gathering the old crowd, and he has all of us looking for you. Give me your direction."

I gave it without hesitation. This despite the fact that though I ached to see Albert, I did not want him to see me—not like this. But I'd been living so long for his return… Only for him.

"Is—is he changed?" I asked.

"Not so much as you."

"When will he come?"

"Dunno, do I?" Danny spat into the gutter. "Right quick, I should think. First thing he did was ask after you."

He loved me. He did, still. Was his love strong enough to survive what I'd become?

The light burgeoning inside me won out. "Tell him—tell him I can't wait to see him."

****

"He's coming here?" Darcy wailed when I returned to our room and told her the news. "You directed him here?"

I sat down next to the bed, where she lay, and took her hand.

"Of course I did."

"But we don't let anyone in here."

"This is Albert," I told her. "Albert."

She eyed me with wonder but did not speak the words that must have hovered on her lips. We had been through so much together, Darcy and me. I should have said we shared the love of family. Perhaps for that reason she kept silent.

"When he gets here," I promised, "we'll go out, walk and talk. Leave you out o' it."

"Won't he want to stay here with you?"

"I don't know."

"He might bring disease from that filthy prison." Contemplating what she'd said, Darcy began to laugh. She kept on laughing till I thought she'd choke, and I joined in.

"Listen to me," she wheezed ruefully when she could again speak. "Put on your good dress, Pol, do."

I hated my good dress, it being the one I'd worn to meet my gentlemen. But I had nothing else even half decent.

Looking into my eyes, Darcy sat up. "Put it on, duck, and I'll brush out your hair. You want to look the best you can."

****

That wait proved harder, almost, than all the rest. Tense, I hovered between joy and dread, anticipating the longed-for bliss of seeing Albert and fearing his reaction when he saw me.

Darcy decided, after all, to go out, so I was alone— alone when the knock fell on the door late that same afternoon. All at once I couldn't breathe. But I hauled the door open anyway, expecting to see Albert, my Albert as he'd looked when we last had parted.

But if I had changed during those three years, he

had also. He would be twenty now, a young man. I saw immediately how he'd grown—even on the poor fare that passed for food inside. His hair had darkened from bright ginger to auburn, and it nearly brushed the lintel of the door. Pale and painfully thin, he looked little more than a skeleton.

But his gaze reached for mine. I looked into his eyes and saw the boy I'd loved all the while. Somehow, by a miracle, he'd kept his light burning steady and strong.

"Polly," he said.

At the sound of his voice—beloved voice!—my eyes flooded with tears, and my throat stopped so I could not speak. I reached for him, drew him in through the doorway by his hands.

And touching him—touching him was sheer heaven, all I could imagine of bliss.

"Oh, Pol," he whispered, and pulled me into his arms.

Warmth enfolded me, comfort such as I'd not known in three years. That despite the fact that beneath his clothes I could feel every rib of him, a rack of bones. I knew in that instant, all in a flash, that if life had been difficult for me these past years, it had been equally hard for him, inside.

Survival.

Would he understand what I'd had to do?

That moment seemed to last forever. At last, though, Albert stirred and took my shoulders between his hands, and looked down at me. "Pol, oh, Pol, what have you done to yourself?"

I began to weep, to sob there against his shoulder. With him so much taller than me now, that shoulder made a good refuge in which to hide my shame. I did not want to see what lay in his eyes, not then.

When I could speak I whispered, "Forgive me. Please forgive me."

"Polly. Polly, look at me."

I couldn't. Gently, he raised my chin with his fingers and met my eyes.

"It ain't your fault. Ain't your fault, girl, understand?"

That made me cry harder. How wide and deep was his heart that he could welcome me in and love me still? Ruined, no longer pretty, dying—for I did not doubt my end. Everything I had done showed in these marks on my face.

"Here, don't weep. I've waited so long to see you. Don't spoil it with tears."

I strove mightily to contain my emotions. For him—I could do anything for him.

"Oh, Albert, what you must think of me—"

"I think you're my Polly, my lovely girl."

"But—"

"It ain't your fault," he said again. "It's mine, all mine. I shouldn't have been so stupid as to get caught. You had nobody looking after you once I went away, did you?"

I shook my head. The events of three years ago now seemed so distant, as if I saw them through a haze. "I couldn't find a job. I tried, Albert. I asked everywhere. I paid the first month's rent, but then Mr. Grimp, he wanted—"

Albert tensed. "Did you give in to him? Was it him did this to you? I'll kill the bastard, so I swear."

"No, I didn't. I left the Close. But then I was on the

street. It was winter. I met Darcy—she's my friend, I live with her now—and she looked after me a while. But times were lean and she knew these gentlemen—"

"She a whore?"

I considered the question. I hated to apply that ugly word to one so dear to me. "She only saw certain men. But we needed money to live, and they paid great sums. For me."

It sounded so lame now, as if I should have been able to keep myself pure for him.

He grunted.

I withdrew from his grasp and looked into his eyes. "I swear, Albert, there weren't many."

"Enough." Very gently, he touched the sore on my cheek. "How long you been like this?"

"A while. It's a slow disease, this. I've been to see a physician, Mr. Richards. He says it takes a long time to—to—"

"Isn't there a cure?" he asked even though he must have known there wasn't. No fool, Albert. He'd always been right quick. I reckoned that was hope talking.

"No. There are treatments, different things folks try." I didn't tell him that I—or more particularly my virtue—had been one of those things, not then. "Nothing seems to help much."

"But it does help? We'll see you right, Polly. I promise that. Whatever it takes."

"You can't go back to the old ways, Albert. You can't get caught again, you simply can't."

He said nothing. I clutched the front of his jacket. "All I want—all I truly want is time for us to be together."

"Then that you shall have."

He wrapped me in his arms, and I felt his love. Albert's heart had remained true to me for all the time we'd been apart.

He loved me still.

Chapter Twenty

As I say, if I had changed while Albert was inside, he had also, a truth I discovered in full during the weeks that followed. I do not mean just physically, though I had trouble reconciling his height, and he had a cough that dogged him like a ragged cur.

Albert had always been patient, with kindness lying beneath his iron will. Now he seemed much quicker to anger and displayed a tendency toward violence I'd never thought to see in him. Not toward me—no, never toward me. But he snapped at the boys, those who flocked to join back up with him. And he seemed ready to square off against any strangers who crossed him.

I supposed he'd learned that in prison, having had to defend and stick up for himself. When I asked him about it—what it had been like inside, I mean—he said, "I don't want to talk about that, Pol. I don't ever want to think about it again. The promise of being with you's wot got me through. That's all I want to remember."

But it frightened—terrified—me to see him picking up the old life again. That had got him into trouble. That had separated us.

"What else do I know?" he asked when I spoke of it. "I need to feed myself. And take care of you."

"If you get picked up, I'll never see you again." I didn't know how long I had. I didn't know how long he'd get.

The meeting between Albert and Darcy—for meet they inevitably did—felt like one part of my life crashing into the other. They first met that very next day when he came to pick me up and go out. Darcy was there, abed and sleeping, but she roused herself and got up, wrapped in a scrap of sheet.

It is a strange truth I've learned that we seldom see those who are dear to us. We might look at them, yes, but we don't *see*. On that morning though, I seemed to see each of them through the other's eyes.

The inspection Albert gave Darcy was cool and appraising. It started at the top of her sorely tangled head and traveled down her poorly clad body, prodding and weighing, only to return in order to perform a minute inspection of her lesions. She looked, so I imagined he thought, like any common streetwalker.

But she'd kept me alive for three years.

Darcy, as I knew, possessed an equally sharp mind when not fogged by her illness. Indeed, she'd been displaying much more confusion of late. But her blue eyes appeared clear as she sized Albert up in similar fashion, and she had no trouble sensing his disdain.

"So you're the glorious Albert, are you?"

He gave that curious grunt of his, nothing more.

"She spoke of you." Darcy jerked her head at me. "All the while. But you needn't sneer at me. You don't seem much yourself."

I felt Albert's ire spark at that, this lad who'd always been so slow to anger. Still, he didn't speak.

"She's yours now." Darcy waved a hand. "I'm glad to hand her over."

She didn't mean that, I thought. Close as we'd

been, she couldn't possibly be so eager to get shed of me.

Albert did speak then. "All right."

"She says she's your wife. D'you know that?"

"Yeah."

"Well then, that makes you her husband, right? Better act like it."

I wanted to stamp my foot, to tell them I could speak for myself. But I wanted even more for them to get along, these two who meant everything to me.

Only later, when Albert and I walked together along the river hand in hand, did I bring up the subject.

"I wish you and Darcy might get along, if only for my sake."

He glared at me. "She's a whore."

I swallowed hard. "So am I."

"No, Pol." He caught my shoulders and turned me to face him. The light—that which now lay buried so deep in his gray eyes—flared and enfolded me. "Not like her."

What was the difference? I wondered. My few customers were the same as Darcy's. But I did not ask the question aloud. I still wanted Albert to think the best of me despite what I'd become.

"Listen," he said, "it's going to be all right. I'll get you medicine. We'll find a cure. You won't end up like her."

"Albert, I went to see a physician, and like I told you, there is no cure."

"None we know about yet, maybe. There will be."

I tried to shake my head, but he captured my face between his hands and stilled me.

"I swear to you, Pol, we'll find a way."

"And what about Darcy?" Would he look after her too? "I can't just abandon her, Albert, when she's been so good to me and while she's so sick."

"Yeah, I see that."

"She took care of me—"

"No, Pol. You banish that thought right out of your head. You took care of yourself because I wasn't there to do it. You're strong, see? You don't need her."

I blinked at him. "She needs me."

"I need you, Pol. I swear to God you're the only thing that kept me alive inside. In the darkest times, the thought of coming back to you was what kept me going."

So maybe I was his light, just as he was mine.

He drew me into his arms, right there in the open. I could feel his strength, that which had nothing to do with muscle or sinew. The strength, like his light, shone from within.

"Tell you what," he said, his voice vibrating right through me. "I'm going to work hard and get us a place of our own. And we're gonna get married proper. Preacher and all."

"Maybe you don't want to marry me now that I'm—"

"Don't say it. I do want to marry you, Pol. It's all I want. And you're gonna get well, hear?"

His belief, so I thought then, might be enough to carry me.

****

I said nothing to Darcy about Albert's plans—did not mention leaving her in a room she likely could not afford to keep on her own. She went out less and less frequently now to see her gentlemen, and she still took the mercury cure though any fool could see it wasn't helping her much.

At night she would whimper and cry out in her sleep. It made me shudder, knowing the path she followed would also be mine to walk.

When Albert came to see me, he refused to linger in the room if she was there. When he called for me, he always made an excuse for us to leave as quick as possible. He spoke to her little and of her even less.

Indeed, he spoke little on any subject. When I prodded him, he admitted a number of the boys had returned to him, and he was "setting up operations." If I protested, he quickly changed the subject to one he thought I'd prefer.

"Pol, I've been sussing out rooms, just for you and me. It won't be anything grand, not at first, but I'm looking for a decent location, like. Certainly better than where you are now."

Invariably, I fretted. "Where will you get the brass?"

"You let me worry about that, love."

He called me that all the time now—love—just like a husband called his wife. I cannot hope to explain how hearing it made me feel…protected and cherished, as if I were the pretty girl with the golden curls once again. As if nothing had changed.

Yet everything had changed.

The first time he tried to kiss me, while walking me home after dark, I protested, "Albert, no. The physician I saw said—well it's not safe, not safe for you."

"I don't care, Pol." I felt a new urgency in his touch. "I love you, and I don't care."

"But I care. That's why—"

He disregarded me and pressed his lips to mine.

That kiss changed my world. Unlike the gentle busses we'd shared in the past before he went inside, this carried heat and sought to possess me in the very best way. It admitted me to him in turn. And just like the sweet kisses he'd given me before, it let me taste his light.

I might have been able to resist anything else. Not that. I let him kiss me till my knees went weak.

He whispered in my ear, "After we're married proper, there'll be more, Pol. Much more."

That night I wept into my blanket. Whatever might happen to me, I didn't want Albert to share this fate of mine.

Chapter Twenty-One

Soon after, Albert came to me and pressed a coin into my hand.

"Pol, I want you to use that to see another physician. I've found a new man. He can cure you. I know he can."

Belief shone in his eyes. Throughout all that followed in the months to come, Albert always held firm to that belief, which seemed curious in one otherwise so shrewd and perceptive.

"What's wrong with the man I saw before?"

"This one's got a reputation for treating—well, the pox. I want you to go."

I went. The physician, a Mr. Ballard, had little in common with Mr. Richards, whom I'd found honest and straightforward. He examined me in a perfunctory manner and promised a cure.

"Truly?" I asked, hope taking hold of me in spite of what Mr. Richards had previously told me.

"Indeed. Your condition is not so far advanced that it cannot be reversed."

"But the other physician I saw—"

"What was his name?"

"Mr. Richards."

"Richards. I know of him." Mr. Ballard scoffed. "Behind the times. I have a medicine of my own devising. It will see you cleared."

I went away relieved of Albert's coin and of a good bit of my dread.

What is happiness? Even lying here surrounded by all this glorious peace, I am not sure I can define it. Suffice to say in the weeks and months that followed, I came as close to it as I ever will. Albert arranged a marriage for us and sorted a little room as well. I fell easily back into letting him sort things—how we would live and eat. How we would share our lives.

It was bliss living with him. Though the room he found us was small and terribly warm, situated at the top of the building, I loved the view from the window and loved that it was ours alone. I thrived on waking in Albert's arms and once more sleeping beside him at night.

I continued seeing Mr. Ballard, who assured me my condition improved, though I could see little change. I felt better, but that might have been due to the balm of Albert's company, the presence of his light always uplifting me.

Mr. Ballard also assured me that so long as I kept on his special medicine, I could not make Albert or anyone else sick. So when Albert's deep kisses moved us to something more, when he possessed me completely—an act bearing absolutely no relation to what I'd endured at the hands of my gentlemen—I made no protest. Albert and I belonged together in that way. We'd been born for each other, and I was his wife.

This is not to say that, even during this happiest of times in my life, I had no worries. They continued to beset me. Sometimes the medicine Mr. Ballard dispensed made me sick. I would vomit and vomit while Albert held the hair out of my face.

Sometimes when I looked at my face in the foggy glass Albert used for shaving and saw the sores still there, I despaired. Then I would think of Darcy, whom I'd left behind in our former lodgings.

I felt guilty about that, especially when, now removed from it all, I went to see her. For I still did slip off to see her when Albert was otherwise engaged. I found her most of the time sprawled atop her cot, and the sight of her shocked me.

It is as I've said—we do not truly see those with whom we associate every day. But now she appeared nothing more than a ravaged skeleton.

I always took her a bit of food or a little money toward the rent, though I did not tell Albert. I didn't even tell him I went there, for he would have objected. Once or twice I took her a drop of my medicine, but not much, for it was terribly dear, and I knew what Albert had to do to earn the price.

Sometimes I found Darcy clear and lucid. Sometimes she raved and barely knew me. I will admit I feared the worst. I wished I could help her, but in my heart I feared her already lost.

My other great worry centered on how Albert made our living. He'd fallen right back into his old ways, and I feared it would end the same as it had before, if not worse.

One night the worry overcame me, and I began weeping. "What if you get taken again?" I hiccoughed the words into his shoulder. "You will never get out of prison."

"Never," he agreed.

That frightened me, right and proper, him agreeing that way. I'd wanted him to deny it, but he said, "Next time, Pol, I reckon I'll swing."

"Hanging?" I gasped. "But they…they don't hang thieves, do they?"

"They do when it's what they call persistent. And I'm not just a thief, am I? I'm head of a thieving ring."

I laid hold of him with both hands. "Then you need to stop! Please, Albert. There must be something else we can do. I'll go out to work. I can start up sewing again."

"That won't cut it, Pol. There's the boys to think of. And you." He kissed me. "There's always you."

"But I can't lose you, Albert. Not again—I wouldn't survive it."

"You won't, love. I promise you won't ever lose me."

But I had once before, and I knew I could again. That most of all had the power to dim the sustaining light.

****

At the end of summer when a troubling suspicion crept into my mind, I took it to Mr. Ballard. He heard me out, listening to all I had to say with a bland expression and shrugged.

"This is only natural, surely? You are a married woman."

"But Mr. Richards—the physician I saw before—told me it would be dangerous for me to get up the duff, for both me and the baby."

"I am not Mr. Richards," he huffed. "And you were not then on a course of my cure."

Hope lit within me. "You're saying it will be all right?"

"Keep taking the medicine, and you should do

well."

"I have new sores, though." I showed him those blossoming on my legs, a foul crop, indeed. "Why would I keep getting them if the cure is working?"

"The cure is sound. Your disease must simply run its course. That is the pox working its way out of your body."

I left having traded more of Albert's coin for a further supply of the cure. But I did not feel convinced. I feared that, unlike Mr. Richards, Mr. Ballard might not be an honest man.

When I told Albert my news, light exploded in his eyes and began to burn sure and steady. He took my hands in his and kissed them, one after the other.

"Are you certain, Pol?"

I nodded.

"Then I'll need to work twice as hard. Not that I mind. This is all I've ever wanted, a proper little family, like, all my own. We'll be right now, love. It's all gone right."

I agreed, and when he kissed me, I kissed him back. But I knew that being a proper family lent no protections. I'd been part of one before, and it had all slipped away.

The next time I went to see Darcy, in September it was, she'd gone from the room. No one knew where. Someone else lived in the room that had been ours.

I felt desperate with worry for her. I went from neighbor to neighbor asking if a corpse had been carried out of there and was directed at length to the tiny Chapel of the Good Shepherd.

The same place where I now lie.

"There's a charity graveyard," one of the neighbors

told me, a girl not unlike Darcy, "for the likes o' us. Not many will touch us, see?" She added, not unkindly, "If she's died on you, duck, she'll be there."

I wanted to tell her I wasn't one of them, not any more. I was married, respectable, on the cure. But looking into her eyes I knew she wouldn't believe it, and I didn't waste the breath.

I went to the chapel, and I spoke to the vicar there. A gentle sort of man, he listened to me patiently and said, "Yes, it's true our mission is to accept for burial those who might not be accepted elsewhere, such as yourself."

There it was again. I said hastily, "Oh, I'm out of that life now. I'm on the cure."

"Are you?"

"Yes. But my friend, Darcy Wilkins she's called, was much worse off than me. Can you tell me, tell me if…?"

"She will not be in the churchyard proper, you understand. Such as she are laid to rest in Spitalfields, right next door. What is that name again? Darcy Wilkins?" He led me to a tiny room furnished with a table and shelves. There he looked through a thick book.

"Some are sent here from the workhouses, some from the prisons. Others arrive nameless. Well not nameless, of course, but no one can tell us their names. I try to record them all. I do not see here the name you have mentioned. But three were brought in last week without known names."

Oh, I ached over that! Had poor Darcy died alone in our room and been carried here without so much as an identity? How could I tell?

"May—may I see the ones who were brought in?"

"I'm sorry, my dear, they've gone into the ground. We do not tarry, you understand. We dare not."

"But I need to know. She was very—very important to me. Was one of them a young girl, about my age?"

Regret filled his mild eyes. "All three were. I am sorry," he repeated.

"Might you at least take me to their graves?"

His expression grew sorrowful. "I'm afraid you don't understand. See the names in this book?" He leafed through the pages. "All these are buried in our little plot of ground. We cannot possibly give them individual graves."

"Then…then how…"

"It is a communal grave, or I should say a series of them."

I shook my head in disbelief or denial.

He looked away from me, bent his gaze hard on the book filled with names and non-names. "Our workers dig large pits, over in the field, that they then reopen time after time. Our dead are laid there. I assure you we do exercise all due respect and say prayers over them."

A pit of a grave shared with many others. Had that been poor Darcy's fate?

Suddenly the vicar brightened. "Clothing."

"I beg your pardon?"

"Before they go into the ground, we strip them down."

"What!" I cried, appalled.

"They do not need their clothing where they lie, child, and the garments can be sold to pay our workers. We are an impoverished parish. The clothing taken from these last three has not yet been sold. Do you think you would recognize your friend's clothing?"

Stunned, I nodded.

"A moment."

He went to the door and called for a woman. A hushed conversation took place there, and I heard footsteps hurry away. Soon enough they returned.

The woman came into the tiny room with what looked like rags in her hands.

"Do you recognize anything here?"

A jumble of clothing it was, so poor I couldn't imagine anyone wearing such garments or wanting to purchase them now. At first, to my relief, I did not recognize any of them. But then I caught a glimpse of pale blue at the center of the bundle.

"There. Her shawl." I drew the tattered object out from among the others, and the vicar did not protest. Mr. Spencer had made Darcy a gift of this shawl long ago—it had been her pride and joy.

Taken from her now, just like her life.

Tears flooded my eyes.

"I am sorry, my dear. Be comforted by the fact that your friend is now free of her disease and at peace."

I wanted that shawl to keep, but I feared I'd have to buy it. And the money Albert gave me was too perilously earned to squander. I needed it for my child.

"Go in peace," the vicar bade me when I left. But there was no peace in imagining Darcy dying in our room alone. I had a good cry when I got home. Later when I shared the news with Albert, he drew me into his arms and held me tight.

"That will never happen to you, Pol."

It was the only time he ever lied to me.

Chapter Twenty-Two

I settled in with my grief as I had before, and life went on. Albert brought me some sewing jobs so I felt useful, and that helped. It made me remember stitching dolls' clothes with Ma and brought her closer to me.

I continued to see Mr. Ballard and to take his cure, though sometimes it made me feel terribly ill. My sores got no worse, and I dared to hope his remedy might be doing its work at last.

Then one morning Albert came home with all his knuckles split open and blood on his face.

Ironically, he kept hours not unlike Darcy's, out with his teams of boys while the world slept, and home at daylight. I knew they'd progressed from picking pockets and cadging from shops to home-breaking. Not grand houses, you understand, like those in the West End, but certainly better off than us. How could I object if it bought my medicine, if it would keep our child fed?

Still, the thought of him getting picked up again fair terrified me. Repeat offenders like Albert did have their necks stretched, and no mistake.

But now he let himself into the room and turned to face me, his expression dark as a cloudy day in January. I could feel his anger—you must understand, so close were we, I could sense most his emotions and he mine. And this anger, once so strange to him, was much more often with him since he'd come out of Newgate.

I stared at him with alarm.

"Albert? What's happened?"

A foolish question. All too clearly he'd either been in a dust-up or had thrashed someone who'd made an attempt to fight back. What I meant by my question was, why?

He inspected me where I lay, hair loose on the pillow, still warm from sleep, and some of the rage drained away out of him.

"You all right, Pol?"

"Yes. But what's all this? You coming home in such a state—"

"Nothing for you to worry about."

"It weren't the coppers, was it?" My worst fear.

But he shook his head.

"Did you get caught by a homeowner?" Sometimes, as I knew, homeowners kept firearms and fired at housebreakers. Why not also engage in fisticuffs?

"I told you, don't worry about it."

I scrambled up from the bed. "How can I not worry? Look at you."

I fetched the basin and a cloth. "Sit down."

He obliged, settling on our one chair. More of his ire slipped away as soon as I laid hands on him.

If Albert had changed in manner since being in prison, these six months had also seen him alter physically. No longer pale and thin, he'd packed some muscle onto the tall frame, and the steely glint in his gray eyes made him a man not to be crossed. His auburn hair had grown long and he wore determination like a second coat.

I sponged away the blood at one corner of his

mouth and from his cheek, revealing a rising bruise.

"You've been scrapping."

He didn't deny it, just watched me while I worked.

"That's not like you, Albert. What's happened?"

At first I didn't think he'd tell me. I bathed the knuckles of one hand and then the other. Suddenly his fingers clenched hard on mine.

"A man defends his own."

That surprised me. Our eyes met for a long moment. I didn't need to ask anything else because I knew—someone of his acquaintance had slagged me off, insulted me. And Albert had defended my honor.

Only I had no honor, not any more. Everything this unknown person said about me was no doubt true.

Tears came to my eyes. I lowered my lashes so he wouldn't see.

"I love you, Pol." He raised my hand to his lips and kissed it fiercely before pulling me onto his knees and wrapping his arms around me tight. "I love you."

"I love you too, Albert."

Several long moments passed. I could feel his heart beating strong against mine. I asked, "Did you kill him?"

He shuddered. I felt it go right through him, and he failed to answer.

"Albert, did you—"

"I shouldn't think so. But he won't speak ill of you again."

"If you kill someone, they'll take you away from me for sure. For good."

"I didn't. I won't."

"Albert"—I tried to broach the subject so often on my mind—"you never used to get so angry. Why now?"

"A man has to fight for what's his. Let's go to bed, Pol."

"But—"

"I love you. Let's go to bed."

****

The next blow came scarcely a week later. I'd just been to see Mr. Ballard the day before and got a new batch of medicine, but I don't suppose I can blame what happened on that even if I might be so inclined.

It started as an ordinary day. Albert had come home as usual and joined me in the bed. Now, with the morning, he still lay fast asleep.

I arose at dawn, mostly because I didn't feel well, not uncommon for me now. The babe lying beneath my heart often made my stomach uneasy, but this felt different. In truth, I'd not felt right since starting the new batch of medicine.

As soon as I was up on my feet, the pains hit. They spread all across my belly and punched me in the small of the back like a kick from a horse.

I sat back down on the edge of the bed and wondered what was wrong. No sooner did the cramps ease than they struck again.

I tried to draw a breath and barely succeeded against the intensity of that pain. Let it be said I was good at tolerating discomfort. Given my disease, I lived with it every day. But this frightened me. Where my usual discomfort had teeth, this had fire.

Something was very much wrong.

"Albert?" I whispered.

He slept on, very much as if my life had not been dealt a mortal blow. But my mind went back, back to my mother lying in our bed at Bishop's Close.

"Albert!"

He came awake, sat up, and stared at me. "What is it, Pol?"

I turned my face to him. What he saw there had him instantly on his feet.

"What's amiss?"

"The child. I think it's our child." I'd seen this before, all of it. Only, Ma had wanted rid of Mr. Grimp's child. I did not want to lose Albert's.

Terrified, I began to weep.

"Here," Albert said. "Lie back. I'll go get someone. Is there anyone?"

I'd sussed out a midwife in our building, and I gave Albert her direction even though I did not want him to leave me. He went running, and I prayed to a God in whom I'd not believed for quite some time. I wept for my child and for Darcy, and for Albert whom I loved more than my own life.

None of it did any good. Nor did the presence of the midwife, a rough sort of woman who nevertheless treated me kindly.

What followed proved as inevitable as the coming of sunrise, though it took far longer. It took all day.

At one point I heard the midwife tell Albert, "Mister, I think you're going to lose her."

And he replied, "No, I'm not. You're going to save her, right?"

"I can't save her. I haven't the skill. Better send for a physician."

Albert did. I learned later that Mr. Ballard refused to come. Another man—a stranger—did come, and as Albert always insisted after, the man clawed me back from the brink of death.

I remember little beyond the moment I lost our child. When I woke again, the room was dark and smelled sharply of blood. Ma stood beside the bed.

A curious thing that I could see her even in the dark. But she wore her own haze of radiance, soft and dim. Maybe the smell of the blood brought her, or maybe I was that close to crossing the void to where she'd gone.

"Well, pet," she said.

"Ma."

I'd forgotten how pretty she was. She hadn't looked like this since the days we were all together. It surprised me how much I looked like her.

"How is it you're here, Ma?"

"I'm never far, Polly."

"That's good. I guess that's good."

"Yes."

"I lost my child."

"I know, pet. It's why I came. Just as well."

How could she say such a thing, she of all people, who knew how it felt?

But she went on, "She would have been born sick, Polly, sick like you."

"She?"

"It was a little girl. She's here with me now, in the Light."

The way she said that last word made it special. *Light.* And I knew what she meant. She meant the radiance—the same Darcy had carried, the same that burned so steady in Albert's eyes. It underlay everything, even the darkness. It surrounded Ma now.

"Take care of her for me till I get there."

"I will."

"Her name is Darcy. You hear? Darcy."

"Wot?" I must have spoken aloud and roused Albert, who slept beside me. He drew me into his arms. "Pol, are you hurting?"

Surprisingly, I wasn't. I felt cushioned on a wave of air, lighter than thought.

"Ma was here."

"Was she?" That startled him.

"Our baby, she was a little girl."

"I know. The midwife said. I didn't want to tell you. I thought—"

"I want to name her Darcy."

"All right."

"She's with Ma now. In the Light. I hope they're both happy."

"Go to sleep, Pol. You're raving."

"I'm not. She's there, and Ma was here to tell me. She really was."

"You're scaring me now, Pol. You are." His arms tightened. "I can't ever lose you. Don't care what I have to do."

But I cared. I cared.

Chapter Twenty-Three

I don't rightly know where people go after they die. Following my talk with Ma, I confess I hoped it was into the Light. All I know is, I'm just lying here in this vast, crowded grave with someone else beneath me, and I'm growing more and more numb.

Soon, I suspect, I won't be able to feel anything at all.

It comes to me now that Darcy must be here somewhere with me, unless she went into one of the other pit graves. I can't sense her. I hope she's moved on.

Will I move on? I hope so. I can't tell why I'm waiting, why the memories still come. But they flood upon me in swift succession.

I am Polly Bridger. Rather, Polly Coward.

For I belong to Albert now and forever. Maybe I've no hope of moving into the light after all. But I still have the light I found always in Albert's eyes, from the very first time he looked at me there in the yard of Bishop's Close.

Sometimes that light dimmed with distance. Sometimes it became clouded by his anger, especially after he came out of prison. No longer clear and sunny, there were times it flickered and nearly died.

But it remained mine till the end, just like his love.

It occurs to me, lying here, maybe the light I saw

always in Albert *was* his love for me.

Oh, what a lovely idea! It's better than having all the pain banished, better than a full stomach, better even than the laughter we shared.

For we did share laughter, even then. Albert insisted on looking after me as I recovered from the loss of our child. I'd shed a lot of blood, and recovery came slowly. In fact, I'm not sure I ever did recover completely.

I remained frail, and the strength would not return. I knew Albert took terrible risks and made sacrifices to get me all I needed—or all he fancied I needed. For in truth I needed only his company.

He stayed with me when he could and paid a woman to look in while he was out working. He brought me delicacies to tempt my appetite and made certain I always had Mr. Ballard's cure.

But the cure stopped working. It was as if my weakness lowered the barriers to my disease and allowed it a fiercer grip. The sores on my legs spread rapidly. I got new ones on the palms of my hands and even on my tongue.

Albert pretended not to see, though I knew he must. Anyone looking into my face must see how the pox ate at the skin, especially around my nose. Perhaps he lied to himself.

I stopped sewing, and Albert brought me no more work. I wanted to stop taking Mr. Ballard's cure, but Albert wouldn't let me. The year moved on, and the world once more grew cold.

How I hate November! So many awful things have happened to me around my birthday. This year true tragedy struck—as if we hadn't had enough.

We were abed and sleeping. That is, Albert slept after his late night out on the pinch. I lay wracked by worry, just thinking—remembering, much as I do now.

Sometimes strange thoughts indeed flickered through my head, and I feared it might be the madness setting in. Folks said that at the end, pox sufferers such as me needed to be tied up, to combat their raving.

I did not want to end so. I did not want Albert to see me that way.

I need not have worried.

I heard them coming from afar off—a great clatter down in the street, loud pounding on the outer door, then feet on the stairs.

I sat up. Albert heard the commotion too and surged up from his pillow.

"Jesus!"

Very little light illuminated the room. By the faint radiance that seemed to come from him, he searched my eyes.

"I'm sorry, Pol. I'm sorry."

"What?"

"There's money under that loose floorboard in the corner. Use it for the rent, long as you can."

A wild pounding erupted on our door. "Police! Open!"

"Oh!" I gasped. "Albert, no!" I clutched at him. I never wanted to let go. "You can't leave me again. You can't—"

"I'm sorry, Pol. So sorry." He touched my cheek. "I love you."

The door came crashing open as the coppers broke in. A squad of uniforms surged upon us, the foremost hollering, "Albert Coward? You are under arrest for grand larceny and for inciting others to thievery."

They laid hold of him then and dragged him from my arms, clear out of the bed. He fought them most valiantly—never a coward, my Albert, despite his name. But they used their cudgels on him. I saw the blood begin to flow, and I saw the agony in his face as he battled to remain with me.

I cried and wailed and clung to him. One of the coppers struck me, to get me off.

Albert went very still then. He looked the man in the eyes and said, "I'll kill you for that."

"Threatening a police officer!" The copper yelped. And they wrestled Albert down without mercy.

I was on my feet by then, sick and shaking so I could barely stand. Of all that had befallen me—all those terrible things—this was worst, seeing him beaten like that, my brave, gallant boy.

"Leave her alone," he growled. "That's my wife."

"Widow, she'll be." The head officer flung me a look. "And not long for this world."

"Let me go with him," I beseeched. "Let me—"

"Off, slag! It's no place for you."

"Polly," Albert called as they hauled him out the door, "remember what I told you. Wait for me. I'll come to you—somehow I'll come. Promise you'll wait!"

I whispered, "I will."

****

I have very little clear memory of what happened after that. Events must have followed as they tend to do even after the worst occurrences—but it felt as if clouds filled my mind.

I was very ill. I stopped taking Mr. Ballard's cure

once I ran out, because I needed the money for food and coal, and because I felt it wasn't helping me all that much anyway. I found Albert's stash beneath the floorboards where he'd said, and paid the rent. Desperate for news, I sent those of his boys I could find to the jail and to the court to find out what they might.

"He's back in Newgate," Danny told me, standing at the door of our room with his cap in his hands. "Slated for an appearance before the justices."

"When?" He had to come back to me and soon. I had money for one more month's rent, if I bought no food or coal. After that I'd be out on the street just like last time, only so much worse off.

Who would have thought it could get worse?

"Hard to say." Danny shrugged unhappily. "It moves slow, does the law."

"Can you go there and see him?" I might be able to spare a little money for Albert's comfort, and I thought I could trust Danny.

But he grimaced. "Me? Go there? Not hardly. The coppers are still rounding up members of the gang. They see me, I'm for it."

I said nothing though my heart sank. I didn't know how long I could cling on, but I held madly to Albert's promise that he'd return.

Danny gave me a long look. "How you set for dosh? I only ask 'cause Al would want me to. You got enough?"

"I'm all right for now. You'll bring me any news, when you hear it?"

"I will. I'll bring it when I can. I need to be careful. But, Miss Polly, by the time I hear word of Al—you may be gone."

God help me, I thought he spoke of me being forced from the room for lack of rent.

That was not what he meant though, not at all.

Chapter Twenty-Four

It turned out the landlord knew Albert, had done some business with him in the past. When it came time for me to pay January's rent, I had barely enough, but he allowed me to stay anyway—out of charity or pity, I know not which.

I suppose I was dying by then. Too weak to do much but lie in our bed day after day, I neither ate nor drank. My chest hurt, and breathing was difficult. Strange fancies moved through my head—bright pictures and imaginings—but Ma never returned.

Instead I saw images of Albert and me together, both of us hale and hearty, walking hand in hand through a place I'd never been. Green this place was, with no trace of fog or coal smoke, so it could not be London. Instead of cobbles, grass stretched at our feet, and all the trees had broken into new leaf.

Best of all a clear, soft light bathed us.

I went there with Albert in my imagination, again and again. At other times I burned with fever. I tossed and turned wildly there in the bed and once came to my senses on the floor, huddled in a cold ball. I had no coal for heat and would not have had the strength to kindle a fire anyway.

Did I dream what followed or did it happen in truth? I think it must have happened, for it led to other events, did it not?

Though I lived for what news Danny might bring of Albert, he never came. Instead, at the end of January, the landlord appeared once more at our door.

I could barely stand then. I remember clutching at the door frame to keep myself upright. I retained a few shreds of clarity—enough to tell me he must have come for the rent.

But he said, "Albert's been sentenced to hang."

"What?" I cocked my head. I couldn't have heard him right.

"He'll hang for his crimes."

What crimes were those? He'd thieved, yes, and incited others to do so. He'd broken into people's homes. But only so he—and I—could live. So he could buy my medicine, that hadn't worked for all his wishing.

What had been his crime? Loving me.

"No," I wailed.

"I don't want you dying here. You'll have to leave."

"But—"

"I've been lenient for Al's sake, but he's not coming back."

He's not coming back.

Yet he'd promised.

I never would have thought I had the strength left to weep, yet tears came from my eyes and rained down. I whispered, "Please…"

"You'll have to get out. Go somewhere else."

"Where?"

"Dunno, do I? Wherever they help the likes o' you."

The likes of me.

"Go to the workhouse. They've physicians there."

"All right." I dug within for some scraps of dignity. I would not have him toss me out. Anyway, it didn't matter what happened to me if Albert was gone.

Hanged.

I'd faced a lot of pain in my life. I'd endured much just this last year. Nothing matched knowing I'd never again bask in the warmth of Albert's light.

"It's snowing," he said. "You can stay the night. But come morning, I want you gone."

I agreed. What else could I do?

I lay in the bed that night and prayed to die. I could see no other choices ahead of me. Even that thought, though, did not stay with me. Sanity came and went, and though I wished for a return to the green world I'd shared with Albert, it never happened.

In the morning I rose up, finding the strength somehow, and gathered my few things—some clothing and, as before, a blanket. I left the room door standing open. Nothing there for me anymore.

I walked to Newgate, also as I had before, and stood in the street yearning for Albert. I wondered if they'd let me see him before he went to the gallows. But a copper came out and chased me off.

I do not recall much that followed. I must have wandered the streets. Though I intended to go to the workhouse, I could not recall how to find it.

People in the street stared at me, some with disdain, some with alarm. There are times from which I remember nothing at all. I suppose I lay insensible in some alley, near death.

At last, I took myself to the Chapel of the Good Shepherd, where I'd once gone seeking Darcy.

I will not say the vicar remembered me. He must see hundreds in my condition, though he did seem a bit surprised I came there on my own. I threw myself on his mercy, and while I dimly recall him protesting, saying they were not a hospital and had no facilities for "those still living," he took me in.

I remember lying on a pallet in a dim room, longing with all my heart for Albert to come walking in, released by some miracle to be with me. That fantasy fair possessed my mind. He would lie down beside me and take my hand in his.

Hello, Pol. Hello, love.

All I might wish.

Curiously, I do not remember the moment of my death. I do recall the sickness all streaming away from me like wisps of cloud after a storm blows through.

Perhaps, I thought, that's what my illness was—just a storm. For I kept right on thinking from that moment until now.

And I remained aware, if by lessening degrees. I heard when the vicar discovered me and when he brought a woman to strip me down and wash me. I was wrapped in my own blanket and lay under an impossibly blue sky while two men with spades worked. I could not feel the cold, but I felt the hard ground beneath me, and I felt it when they lowered me down upon those who lie here beneath me now. Others—two of them, I believe—were placed in after, one with an arm flung over my scarred shins, before the dirt came in.

Before that happened, they took my blanket. Even that was not left to me. But I don't suppose I will need it again.

It's peaceful here, and quiet considering how many others lie in this grave along with me. Do they have their thoughts also, separate yet somehow all one?

I wait as I have waited before, running all the events of my life through my thoughts over and over again. But I can no longer feel my limbs so easily, and those events grow ever more distant.

I must remember. I must remember Albert. He promised he would come.

Time trickles by like the river, unmeasured.

****

I cannot see the light. I get to thinking maybe it was never there, a lie despite what Ma said to me after my baby died. Only I don't think Ma would lie to me. I didn't think Albert would lie to me either. But he doesn't come.

It is very dark here, a comforting darkness, but oh, how I long for the light!

It seems I have chased it always, a brightness caught by glimpses in Ma's face when she used to tuck me in, and in Pa's smile. I'd seen it burning banked and low behind Darcy's eyes. Albert had gifted it to me. I'd sought always to capture it for my own, to live on it, to let it lift me above the struggles of every day. This tarnished light may be filtered, it may be sullied and dirty with coal smoke. Yet I desire it still.

Above me, the shovels scrape. I feel rather than hear them, for I can hear nothing now. The dirt above us thins as it is shoveled away. I stare upward with sightless eyes.

A body comes down upon us, a great weight tossed in. It lands beside me with a jarring thud. Its shoulder and head land next to mine. Naked as I, and freshly dead. Another to keep us company.

The dirt comes in. The two workers ignore our presence—to them this is just a chore. Those who lie here mean nothing, are nothing.

But I matter. I mattered to Albert. I matter to him still.

In the new dark stillness, a hand reaches for mine. Fingers enfold my fingers with a familiarity that pierces me right through.

Ah! I should have known. I should have believed he would keep his promise and return to me. I *did* believe. This—this was why I had waited.

The light comes in a rush—warm, consuming, and vibrant. It bathes and uplifts us together so we are able to rise.

Joy comes with it, and I turn to look at him. Hale and hearty, the remnants of the noose still around his neck, he smiles at me as I've not seen him smile in such a long while.

I smile back. Joy radiates from him to me and back again.

Polly, love, I told you I'd come.

Together, we step into the Light.

A word about the author…

Multi-award-winning author Laura Strickland delights in time traveling to the past and searching out settings for her books, be they Historical Romance, Steampunk, or something in between. Her first Scottish Historical hero, Devil Black, battled his way onto the publishing scene in 2013, and the author has never looked back.

Nor has she tapped the limits of her imagination. Venturing beyond Historical and Contemporary Romance, she created a new world with her ground-breaking Buffalo Steampunk Adventure series set in her native city in Western New York.

Married and the parent of one grown daughter, Laura has also been privileged to mother a number of very special rescue dogs, and is intensely interested in animal welfare. Her love of dogs, and her lifelong interest in Celtic history, magic, and music, are all reflected in her writing. Laura's mantra is Lore, Legend, Love, and she wouldn't have it any other way.

Thank you for purchasing
this publication of The Wild Rose Press, Inc.

For questions or more information
contact us at
info@thewildrosepress.com.

The Wild Rose Press, Inc.
www.thewildrosepress.com